Addictive

Love

D. A. Greene

ADDICTIVE LOVE

Greenelight Publishing. First Edition: October 2010
For more information, visit
www.greenelightpublishing.com

This book is a work of fiction. All characters, names, places,
organizations, and events portrayed in this novel either are
figments of the author's imagination or are used fictitiously.

Cover Design by Dana A. Greene
Cover photo by George Doyle/Stockbyte/Getty Images
Author photo by Jeff Brooks

DEDICATION

This book is dedicated to those who tried to break free, but couldn't.

I feel your pain.

ACKNOWLEDGEMENTS

I would like to acknowledge my family and friends who stood by me and put up with me while I brought my dreams to reality. This process has been painful and time-consuming, and you've experienced it all with me. I know you had to deal with many long days, lonely nights, and persistent questioning – like, "How does this look?" from me. You never complained, you never rolled your eyes, and you never undermined my efforts to get here.

Always my personal pep squad – I thank you all.

"The course of true love never did run smooth."

William Shakespeare

"A Midsummer Night's Dream"

"Carved in chocolate."
Nia

Chapter One:
Niani

There are moments in life when even though a person should be focusing on the problems that lie before them, they instead waste precious moments wallowing in the past and asking themselves, "When did it start to go wrong?"

Sometimes, you can pinpoint the exact moment when everything began to crumble slowly in your hands. Like a piece of cake left exposed on the kitchen counter for too long.

Sometimes, it's a word, or an action, or even a look that ignites an unstable situation and causes a volatile reaction. It disintegrates everything so quickly, that the only things you can salvage are the smoke and ashes of what used to be.

Sometimes the events are so small, so obscure, that they slowly and discreetly chip away at the surface of your life until, in time, all you are left with is a fraction of what you once held.

Why do we do this?

I think people relive these moments in a

desperate, last-minute effort to make everything better – as if by figuring out where they went wrong, they can find a solution to put things right again.

Or maybe they simply want to take that information and file it in the section of their mental folders, "HOW NOT TO SCREW THINGS UP NEXT TIME," for future reference.

A small part of me believes we secretly hope that by pinpointing that one specific transgression, we can replay it over and over again in our minds, spinning it magically in circles until—poof—it never happened.

I'm not sure why people do this.

All I know is that right now, that's exactly what I'm doing. I'm trying very hard to figure out when it did indeed start to go wrong.

But at this second, at this speed, and at this location, I really need to be focused on what lies ahead of me.

How did I get here?

My mind works double-time trying to figure that out.

I had been looking forward to this day for some time. It wasn't supposed to end like this. Especially since, it started out so well. If I wasn't so stressed from the current state of things, I could almost smile at the thought of my last 14 hours with Cameron.

Cameron.

His name alone causes my mind to cloud; my heart to race. Even under stress, my body responds to the thought of him.

Cameron.

"If only he...Shit!"

My IPhone went off again. The ringer was

silent, but the light from the screen was enough to get my attention.

It illuminates the inside of my car; it makes me jump.

I already know who it is.

My mind starts to wander again as I remember the day's events that led me here. Scheming like a hustler. Speeding like a lunatic.

Heading towards an uncertain end to a disastrous night.

Less than twenty-four hours before, I was on my way to downtown Baltimore – to accompany Cameron to his best friend's cookout.

Anxious, I kept glancing in the rear view mirror that was angled towards my face. I had to make sure that my makeup stayed in place. That my lips weren't dry. That my hair held its shape.

That everything was perfect.

It had been more than two weeks since we last saw each other, and I wanted to look my best.

This was going to be my first cookout of the summer. Unfortunately, it was being hosted by Kevin. One of the most obnoxious men I've ever met, Kevin is Cameron's best friend and a fellow police officer. I wasn't excited about being around that man, but it was worth it to spend more time with Cameron.

Nervous with anticipation, I chewed my bottom lip. Almost giddy with excitement, I looked out my windshield into the world through a warm yellow light.

Yellow. A sign of my mood. A glow only I was seeing.

Synesthesia.

Some people have this gift – or defect.

They see colors associated with certain sounds, things, smells, or emotions. I'm one of those people. The corneas to my eyes are like the screen to an old television. The tint adjusts with my feelings. Calm, quiet, even depressing days have a hint of light blue. Days when I'm very upbeat or happy have an aura of yellow. Moments of intense feelings, like anger, coat my world in red.

As a child, I used to express my ability innocently to others. Numerous confused and concerned looks from strangers and family, coupled with the realization that no one around me possessed this ability, eventually lead to the wisdom to keep this to myself.

Humidity blanketed the earth and covered the atmosphere with a misty haze. The "dog-days" of summer were in full effect, but I tried my best to look perfect. I left my short hair in its natural state of tight curls. I had enough experience with Maryland summers to know that trying to hold on to a wrap in this weather would definitely be an attempt at futility. It wouldn't take long before my Halle creation turned into a Winehouse disaster.

Besides, no matter what the season, my hairstyle wasn't going to last long. Cameron never failed to work out even my most resilient 'dos. As always, I came prepared.

Just in case.

Pulling in front of his townhouse, I started to get the flutters again. This feeling deep in the pit of my stomach. It feels as though I'm walking a tightrope two stories above the ocean. Trying to avoid a pending fall. I get that feeling whenever I first see him – as if it's our first date all over again. It's been over a year since that first night, but something about him shakes me up every time.

I put my car in park and grabbed my phone on the passenger seat. I called to let him know that I was out front. This was his cue to open the door before I stepped out of the car. (Far be it from me to wait outside in this heat.)

He hates when I do that. Thinks it's somehow lazy and disrespectful that I can't bother to ring the doorbell. He complains every time. This time, he added a line about me being spoiled. I let him know what I thought of his opinion by hanging up in his ear. A few seconds had passed and I started to think I went too far. Just as I went to press redial, I noticed the door was open. He was standing in the doorway.

Stepping out onto the pavement, I struggled to maintain my composure at the sight of him.

Carved in chocolate.

That's what I thought when he opened the door.

That's what I thought the day I met him.

That's what I think every time I see him.

His features mislead you to think he's not from around here. That his words will ring with the hint of an accent. His small, Asian-like eyes, high cheekbones, defined nose, and full lips give him an exotic appearance. His skin, the color of dark chocolate, possesses a smooth, satiny appearance – never greasy, never ashy. His broad shoulders, muscular build, and 6'4" frame complement his chiseled features.

Could have been a model, but in my opinion, he makes a better police officer. He walks, speaks, and moves with an air of authority.

And Lord, his smell!

The pheromones this man emits put my X chromosomes on high alert.

He stood in the doorway wearing a clean, white wife-beater and a pair of distressed jean shorts. Shape up and moustache freshly done. His hair, cut low. Even-Steven. His muscles, perfectly defined. A lesson in anatomy.

I would have passed Anatomy 101 the first time had he been my subject to study. Every muscle name would have been permanently committed to memory.

Shaking his spell, I played off my reaction to seeing him, as I strolled slowly, seductively to the house. Giving him time to take in my curves. Appreciate the view of my legs in heels. Notice the men on the corner, who stopped their conversations to look in my direction.

Once inside, I rolled my eyes and let him know I didn't appreciate the spoiled comment. He responded by smiling and giving me his nonchalant, flipping motion of the hand.

That always irritates me.

Having somewhat of a "Short Man syndrome", I hate being disregarded in anyway. That one motion made me want to take my 5-foot-nothing body, do a 2-foot vertical leap, and knock that smirk off his big head.

Seeing that he'd won our ongoing game of wills by making me lose my cool first, he smiled. He gathered me up in his arms—notably without effort—and kissed me.

"You know I love it when you get mad. You're so feisty for such a little thing," he said.

That small effort melted my anger like butter. His warm touch and deep voice worked instantly to calm my emotions. Not to be outdone, I managed to rustle up some mild irritation for the "little thing" comment.

"Put me down! You think 'cause you're like twice my size, you can just do whatever."

I started wiggling to break free of his hypnotic embrace. The heat from his body was making me lose focus. I hated the spell he had over me. Every encounter was a fight not to give in to my feelings.

"I'm not your child."

"Yeah, but I'm your daddy, though. Isn't that right?" He set me back on my feet. "Or did my ears deceive me the last time you were here?"

Another roll of the eyes.

"Whatever, *boy*!"

I pushed past him and made my way to the couch.

I knew I'd touched a nerve by calling him "boy". Blessed with an easy-going nature, this was one the few pet peeves he had. I had him by four years, but being a male in his twenties, four years was equivalent to eight. In my mind, this gave me the authority to address him as his elder whenever the mood dictated. I loved to challenge his maturity if I felt the need. This was my ace in the hole. His Achilles heel.

"Come on, shorty. You know I'm hardly a boy. Stop playing with me." A small amount of tension laced his words.

I won round two.

"So, you're driving, right?"

My flash temper ignited again. Instant attitude developed.

"*I know he didn't just ask me if I was driving,*" I thought.

My temper was as short as my stature. With a role of the eyes and a turn of my head, I proceeded to lay into him.

"Uh, *WHY* would I drive when *YOU* invited me, and this is *YOUR* friend's thing, *AND* I already drove all the way up here from..."

"All right, shorty. Chill! Chill! I was just kiddin'. You know I'm driving."

He dominated the third round. I was one hit away from a TKO.

I closed my mouth and tried to play it off. I pretended I knew he was testing me and sat down while he went upstairs to finish getting dressed.

There was no harm meant in the word "shorty." One of his many terms of endearment for me, it's a typical pet name from men in this area. Being from Baltimore, he pronounces it "shor-ty", while my Prince Georges County and D.C.-residing brothers pronounce it more like "shaw-ty." (I still need to get used to his version of slang without considering him a "ba-ma".)

I glanced around his first floor and noticed a welcome change in scenery. The area had recently been cleaned. The carpet still held the wheel imprints from a vacuum. The wall mirror was crystal-clear. Its frame had been dusted. The scent of Clorox and Carpet Fresh filled the room. This was a far cry from its usual state. (He claims to be a neat-freak on his days off. I have yet to witness it enough times to believe him.)

His home décor was typical hood-classy. A combination of tacky and tasteful. From the first date, I've wanted to give him a few decorating tips for his bachelor pad, but kept it to myself.

End table, coffee table, and entertainment center made of Italian black lacquer with gold trimming. Black leather sofa with some animal print throw blanket folded over the back. Gas fireplace framed in black marble. African-themed statues on the mantle enclosing pictures of him and his family.

No children. A rarity for a 25-year-old male in this area.

My eyes went back to the fireplace. A chill shot through my body as I received flashbacks of the first of many nights in front of it.

I was sprung from day one.

The scent of him carried down the steps before his physical presence did. The warm smell of Hanae Mori emitting from his skin forced me to close my eyes and reminisce. Another flashback entered my mind. Out of pure reflex, the memory signaled circulation to a certain area – preparing it for the expected.

Feeling his eyes on me, I leaned towards his sofa table, pretending I wanted a closer inspection of the pictures perched on top. He walked right behind me and leaned forward - playing along.

I deliberately wore a short skirt on a mission today. His crotch pressed right up against me. I could feel the thick texture of his jeans through the soft fabric of my panties.

"What are you looking at?"

"This picture of you as a baby. You were so cute."

I looked back at the picture in the gold frame. A handsome, cinnamon-brown woman in a beige headband, sleeveless white top, and acid-wash jeans sat holding a cherub-faced, toothless, smiling infant. Her hair was in a thick, reddish-brown mushroom. The baby had a patch of black, curly hair on the top of his chubby, mocha skin. The more I looked at her face, the more I realized the woman was still a girl – not yet out of her teens. They both looked happy and innocent in this picture.

His hands slid down the side of my thighs, then up beneath my skirt. He grabbed my hips and firmly squeezed. "What do you mean 'were'?"

"Just what I said, Big Foot. You *were* cute."

Big Foot was a crack at his height and hairiness.

He leaned over until he was right at my ear. My spot. One of them at least.

"So what am I now?" He said in a low, breathy whisper. He pulled my hips closer and started to grind slowly.

"Uh...I...don't...I'm not..."

God, that massive bulge in his pants! Made it so hard to concentrate. Warmth began in the pit of my stomach. From a pinpoint center, it spread out to cover my entire body. A sensual chill followed the warmth – causing gooseflesh to erupt in a wave.

"Huh? What was that? I didn't quite hear you," he said smugly.

It had been more than two weeks since I last felt him. At that moment, it felt like two years. I wanted him to move that thin layer of cloth to the side. There was no more use for it. It was getting soaked. All of its absorptive capabilities were exhausted.

I was riding a fantasy. Praying that he would join me. I wanted him to release that bulge from its prison. Release me from mine.

Take me just...like...this.

He ended that dream with a chaste kiss to my cheek.

"Come on, babygirl. We're already late. I wanna get there while they still have some food left."

"*Damn! Teasing me again. How can someone so young have so much control?*" I thought.

He always surprised me.

I composed my emotions and brushed it off
like dandruff.

"Sure thing. Just let me go potty, first."

Yeah, I had to dry myself off. This was
going to be a long day.

The drive to his friend's house was shorter
than expected. Though not as nice as Cameron's
neighborhood, near the University of Maryland,
this area had its own appeal. The townhouses
were older and sat on small hills. Each house
had its own flight of stairs on the hills. Some had
two. These stairs led to more stairs that led to
weathered porches.

Each set of stairs was cracked and warped
in its own distinct way. The elements, the shift-
ing of the earth's crust, and time all did their job
on the concrete. Like fingerprints, no two sets of
stairs were the same. I imagined having to lug
groceries, a new TV, or even a baby carrier up
those steps. The image alone made me grateful
for the elevator in my complex.

This area of houses reminded me of the
ones that grace the quieter suburbs of Northeast
D.C.

It reminded me of home.

I tried to make myself think that I was just
off South Dakota Ave instead of somewhere off
Caton Ave. The unknown brings about fear. I
tried to find the familiar in the unfamiliar. A
warm feeling took over and settled my growing
nerves.

Being in Baltimore always made me a little

anxious. Not that I'm afraid of the hood – it's just that it's is not my hood. I'd rather run through Anacostia Park at midnight wearing nothing but my Vickies, than walk through Park Heights in the middle of the day, covered head to toe. And, I know there are people in Baltimore hoods that feel the same way about D.C.

Kevin's house looked like one of the many brick houses with white wooden porches, except his porch was screened in. The yard was lined with several bushes and flowers. Not neatly manicured like the residential landscapes in Woodmore, but still lovingly tended to. I was slightly impressed by Kevin's house.

"Yo! Don't leave any cigarette butts in the yard. My moms'll kick your ass and my mine."

Correction, Kevin's mother's house.

A short man with a pecan complexion and a huge grin approached the car with a beer in hand. His handsome smile was more noticeable, sans moustache. The dimple in his chin stood out on his cleanly-shaven face. Kevin was unquestionably attractive. A shorter, lighter version of Lance Gross, he had one of the best bodies this side of Maryland. Toned and nicely cut. Perfect skin. His only flaws being his height and cocky attitude. What he lacked in height, he compensated for with his loud personality – and, as word has it, he made up for that in the bedroom. His random flings loved to brag about the size of his package, as if it justified his treatment of them.

As small as he was, I used to wonder how he could end up one of Baltimore's finest. (Who was he going to protect if he was barely taller than me?) Guess you couldn't penalize someone for genetics, at least not in the workforce of the 21st century – not without litigation, anyway.

His normally bright, honey-brown eyes had a glassy look to them.   His smile was slightly crooked and he was sweating more than usual. He didn't need to open his mouth, for me to tell he was drunk, high, or both. This meant that he was going to be extra loud and extra obnoxious. Whatever "flavor-of-the-week" chick at his coo-kout would be taking the brunt of this transfor-mation.

These women, whose names I could never remember, always perplexed me. They seemed so eager to be with him that they put up with even his most degrading comments. He seemed equal-ly as eager to use any opportunity to disrespect them.   It was as though he felt that keeping a bunch of females and publicly demeaning them made him a "bigger" man, so to speak.

Napoleon complex came in all forms.

I felt sorry for them both.

"What's up, 'Rique?"

Tyrique, Cameron's middle name, was ob-viously the more ghetto choice than his first name. By either his decision, or just the nature of the streets, most of his friends called him Tyri-que or 'Rique for short. They sometimes called him Rico or – my least favorite – Rico Suave.

Only twice, have I noticed his friends call-ing him this, but both times irked the hell out of me.   His friends had this sly smile as they dragged the name out, practically singing "Ri-COOOO Swa-VEEEE." Cameron responded, but had this embarrassed, slightly irritated look. Ac-cording to him, Rico Suave was the name he took in high school because he thought he was a play-er. But given the way that his boys said it, I al-ways wonder how much dirt he did to earn that title.

Cameron and Kevin locked hands and embraced each other in the typical male fashion – with the "oh-so-macho" fist-pound to the back.

"Bout time you got here, Nigga! You just missed it. You know Trina, right? Shawnte was about to light into Trina's ass when she saw her talking to Dante out back. I was all ready for the main event, but then Shawnte's sister asked me to intervene. So then, I had to turn into the damn officer of the law and act like I was breaking it up and shit, just so Trina wouldn't get her ass beat."

"Man, Dante and Shawn always got some drama with them."

"Yeah, and remember Ceez? He just got back from Iraq last week. He up in this bitch looking depressed like a motherfucka! His moms say it's just the adjustment and all, but peep this...Jay told me his wife is pregnant by some clown that work down at the post office! Yo! Can you believe that shit? We need to take that nigga out, and get him some pussy or something. He so in love, Jay told me that he told him that he was going to work it out with her and help raise the baby and shit. 'Cause he love her, and he know how hard it was on her with him being gone, blah-blah-blah!"

"For real, Yo? Damn!"

"Lord, men gossip worse than females," I thought. *"And does he have to curse so much?"*

Since I have my own potty-mouth to deal with, I normally don't get offended easily. But his frequent use of profanity and the N-word almost made me blush.

"Awww, man, and Fats! THIS nigga threw up on himself in the basement, and everybody act like they ain't never seen fuckin' vomit before and shit, so nooo-one tried to help me! Even Andy's bitch-ass had the nerve to be like, 'Yo, I would help, but my girl just got me this shirt.' So, I had to practically drag that chunky nigga up the steps by myself. Can you imagine what that shit was like? Fuck! Dude need to wash his ass once in awhile. Man, I was so fuckin' pissed that I kicked everyone out the den and made them go outside in the heat – like they was on punishment and shit!"

Kevin and Cameron shared a good laugh at that. Even I let a smile escape. The thought of grown folks being sent outside to play – like when your mother sent you out for messing up the house – made me want to chuckle. To keep from encouraging Kevin, though, I kept it in. He loved attention – especially from women.

I don't hate Kevin, per se. It's just that whenever Cameron's around him, he seems to get a little louder, a little more obnoxious, and the rate of profane words to normal ones kicks up a notch or two. The result of competing male hormones.

My mom always says, "Testosterone is a catalyst that amplifies the negative traits in men. The more they have around, the more unpleasant they become."

Plus, I always feel a bit uneasy around Kevin, as if I were a doe in the clearing, and a predator was hiding in nearby cover.

A woman came over to the car carrying a big bag filled with various kinds of alcohol. I didn't realize at first, but this was Kevin's flavor of the week. At first glance, I couldn't see why.

She was 5'5", about an inch taller than Kevin. Her two sizes too small attire was riddled with VBL's and VPL's – Visible Bra Lines and Visible Panty Lines. Her shape was awkward, at best. She was thick, but not in an attractive, proportioned way. In fact, it seemed that most of her thickness was focused around her gut that was protruding out of a tight white tank top and white skinny jeans. Her breasts were modest—a B-cup, like mine—but they were deflated and looked too small on her thick body. Her butt stuck out, but it flattened at the bottom. Almost formed a square. She had no hips, but thick thighs. Fat arms, but skinny legs. A chin and a half that was bordering on a double.

I gave her the benefit of the doubt and attributed her electrified-chicken hairdo to the heat and humidity of the season, but the ragged, uneven split-ends made me itch to start trimming.

Despite all of her imperfections, her face was pretty. Gray eyes, a small, button-nose, and full lips. The most flawless beige skin that I've ever seen.

Regrettably, her outfit was completely unflattering. It accentuated the negative while de-emphasizing the positive. Her pretty face was her only redeeming factor.

Gray, feline-like eyes made her seem as if she was all stank-attitude, but she greeted me with an unexpectedly warm smile.

"Hi, I'm Trina."

The girl from Kevin's story.

"*Poor thing*", I thought. "*Kevin really was a trifling!*"

Cameron put his arm around me and flashed his 100-watt smile. I struggled not to beam with pride at his subtle act of possession.

"What's up, Trina? I see Kevin's got you working already. This is Niani. Niani, this is Trina."

My pride deflated at the fact that he didn't give me a title. Just "Niani." Avoided a label. Something that would denote commitment. I tried hard not to be insulted. At least he was smart enough not to introduce me as his friend.

Ignoring the sting of his introduction, I reached out to grab Trina's extended hand and replied, through slightly tight lips.

"Nice to meet you, Trina."

Trina quickly ended the handshake in order to gain control of her bag before the contents hit the sidewalk. I looked to Cameron for some male chivalry.

"Cam, are you going to help her with her bag or just wait until it falls?"

Cameron grabbed the large bag with one arm, as Trina smiled with gratitude. She rubbed her arms with relief and looked back towards Kevin.

Kevin was halfway up the steps carrying the same Corona bottle he brought on the way down.

The cookout was more fun than I'd anticipated. Cameron and his friends entertained the group with jokes and trash-talking. The funny stories about high school and the even funnier stories about dumb criminals had me dying most of the evening. Then, along came the raggin' or clownin' – whatever they call it up there. The alcohol and competing testosterone had the men cutting on each other so much, I felt like I was watching a Kevin Hart special.

One poor soul, who wore the worst fake platinum Jesus-piece I've seen in my life, was the main target for most of the afternoon. The chain was too unrealistically thick to be platinum. The actual piece was the worst likeness of Jesus I ever created in jewelry-form. "Jesus" looked more like an emaciated George Clooney on a cross. The expression on his face, which I assumed was intended to be one of suffering, was a cross between boredom and mild indigestion. To top it off, the cross was imposed over some kind of small house or stable. I almost peed in my pants when his friend, Leon, told him that he was going to hell for keeping Jesus in an outhouse.

Kevin sent Trina back and forth to the store for liquor runs. Being the superficial asshole that he was, I initially wondered what he was doing with her. By the end of the night, I knew why – she paid for everything. She also worked the grill and did most of the clean up after it was over.

By one in the morning, most of the people had left. There were a few couples bunned-up in the basement, and Fats was still passed out on the lawn. The four of us—Cameron, Kevin, Trina, and I—were sitting on the back porch drinking. Trina and Kevin were talking shit to each other, while Cameron and I watched the show.

My tolerance for alcohol is low, but I let Trina talk me into drinking two bottles of Smirnoff Ice. The combination of the alcohol and muggy atmosphere made me too warm for comfort. The constant assault of mosquitoes added to my irritation. A night like this would have had me running for the comfort of my own bed, but I dealt with it for the pleasure of his company. I dabbed at my forehead and slapped at my legs while trying to stay awake.

"Whatever, Trina! You know you sprung off this dick. That's the reason I got your ass up in this camp working like a field slave. You lucky I let you have some every once in a while."

"Negro, please! Like I don't be having your little ass biting the sheets hollerin' for your mama. Last night he called my name in the perfect note of C, and this nigga can't carry a tune to save his life!"

"Yeah, you do be getting' them kids up out of me. You got a mouth like a Hoover vac."

Cameron and Kevin shared a laugh and a hand slap across the table. I looked away – slightly ashamed for her. Kevin degraded her with no thought to who was around. Trina however, wasn't fazed.

"Don't be actin' like you don't go down on me."

"What? When?" He stood up, hitting the table and spilling his Remy VSOP and Coke. Like a trained seal, Trina grabbed a napkin and started wiping the spill without missing a beat.

A sound of heavy breathing and footsteps caught everyone's attention. In unison, we turned to the direction of the sound, only to see Fats struggling to get up. Pieces of dead grass clung to the back of his neck and matted locks. Chunks of vomit stuck to the dark stain on the front of his dirty white tee. He stumbled towards the gate with his eyes closed. Cameron and Kevin shook their heads and turned around, as if this was nothing new. Trina finished her story.

"You remember that night after your shift. You said you were too tired to do it, but then, I came downstairs with some whipped cream and cherries and nothing else but my thong on."

Cameron scrunched up his face, leaned in to my ear, and said "Ewww!"

It came out a lot louder than it should have. I had to cover my mouth to keep from laughing aloud. The alcohol was making it harder to control my actions, as it was obviously affecting his ability to be discreet.

She glanced in our direction as if she heard something, but kept right on talking.

"You didn't ask any questions then!" A look of triumph was on her face.

Kevin swiped both his hands in her direction in a "whatever" motion.

"Bitch, I was high!"

I winced at the b-word. Cameron looked at me as if he knew I would be offended.

"I had the munchies so bad that if you put whipped cream on your pimple, I would've sucked the pus out of it. Anyway, I don't remember that shit, so it don't count!"

"Oh, so you don't remember me sitting on your face and you slurping away like I was drenched in hot sauce?"

"Ewww!" Cameron said, not even bothering to try to whisper this time.

She glanced at us again with a quick, embarrassed expression, but continued their "meaningful" discussion.

Cameron leaned in again.

"Yo, is it the alcohol, or does she have, like, a five-o-clock shadow going on? I'm going to have to clown Kevin about this. She's starting to resemble Fred Flintstone."

I snickered and almost spit a mouthful of Smirnoff onto the table. I knew it wasn't right to laugh, but I couldn't help it. I tried my best to contain it as much as possible because I didn't want her to think we were talking about her – even though, we were. (At least, Cameron was.)

He was so close to my ear, the vibrations from his deep voice made my earlobe tickle.

Somewhere in the middle of his jokes, he leaned closer so that his lips barely grazed my ear as he spoke. The tickle he created traveled down my neck towards my stomach. Instead of making me want to laugh, it made my breathing irregular. I started to feel that warmth again. Slowly, I closed my eyes against the sensation.

Cameron sensed what was happening and put his hand on my upper thigh, massaging dangerously close to the hot zone.

"Are you getting sleepy?" he whispered.

"Uh-huh," I replied, barely able to breathe.

"You ready to go?"

"Uh-huh."

Far off in a distant place, I could hear Trina still arguing.

"...told that nigga not to call me again, and it wasn't even like that! You the one who be sweating..."

She stopped mid-sentence, which made me open my eyes. I saw her staring at us affectionately, almost enviously.

"You know what? You two make a really cute couple."

She smiled and returned to her drunken rant, as if nothing had interrupted it.

Cameron took his hand off my thigh and pulled back. We both smiled at each other, but an awkward silence settled in the small distance between my mouth and his. A dark knowledge entered my mind and made me shift uncomfortably. He acknowledged my thought, but abruptly restored the mood by kissing me.

Every parting of his lips and every probe of his tongue helped to push away the nagging thoughts in my head. Every transfusion of sweet, alcohol-tinged saliva worked to clean away any negative energy. Wash away any guilt.

I pulled away from him and looked in his eyes. Thankful for the reprieve he just gave. The thoughts were still there, but they were far away. Instead of creating a sharp pain in my heart, they only left a dull ache. Even that had started to dissipate.

He rubbed his hand through my hair and then, lovingly down my face.

"Let's go back to my house."

The ride to his place was short. Too short. The Smirnoff had me tipsy beyond reason, and I was out in minutes. I dreamt about my grandmother's house in Northeast, DC. I dreamt of home:

It was summertime and scorching hot outside, but the small window AC unit kept the first floor so cold, you could see the frosty air escaping from the vents. Bob Barker was hyping up a heavyset female contestant over a wooden bedroom set prize, while the horns from the theme song blared through the TV console. I sat on my grandma's lap, watching daytime TV and waiting for my mother to pick me up after work.

Shouts of "Red light! Green light!" could be heard faintly over "The Price is Right." My twin cousins, Adrian and Eddie, were playing outside in the mind-numbing heat and humidity.

But it was blissfully cool in grandma's lap.

I sat up and looked into her beautiful, weathered face. She had her hair like mine: parted down the middle, two long braids, ending at her shoulder blades. At 70 years old, her slightly wavy, jet-black hair barely showed any gray. My sandy-brown, tightly curled hair had glints of blond from the season's sun.

She took a long pull of her Newport and blew the smoke out the side of her mouth, away from my face; all the while, never taking her eyes off me. Lovingly fanning the smoke away, she smiled. I grinned in return, so hard that my face hurt. My tongue probed the empty socket where my baby front tooth used to be. Then, I frowned.

"Gramma, you sure it's okay for you to be watching me today? You're dead."

"Baby, no matter where I am or what I am, I'll always be watching you. Don't you worry, not one little bit."

I smiled again and rested my head on her shoulder – my nose touching her neck.

I was six years old, and I had my "Gramma" with me. She kept me cool in the summer. Made sure I was sweating-warm in the winter. She rocked me back to sanity when I cried hysterically for my mother. She scolded me for coming in and out of the house too many times. She scolded my mom for raising her hand to me in the same manner that she raised her own to "light" my mother's "tail" – as she called it. She wrapped her bony arms around my waist and pulled me closer into the safety of her own body.

I was twenty-nine years old.

All of a sudden, we were the same height, but I still fit comfortably in her lap. I sniffed the soft, loose folds of her throat, amazed at how strong she was. The scent of Gloria Vanderbilt, Shower-2-Shower, and some faint medicinal smell brought feelings of peace to my tired grown body. I smiled even harder than before as tears of joy escaped my closed eyelids.

Then, I felt something warm on my thigh.
A hand.

It was rough and calloused. It inched closer towards the hem of my jean skirt.

Instantly, I knew fear.

I didn't want this touch.

I held on tighter to my grandma. She held on tighter to me.

But the hands were stronger than Grandma's thin arms. Suddenly, holding on to her was like trying to hold on to a crumbling sand castle. The surface of her body slid away in tiny particles of matter.

The hands lifted me up, but I felt a sensation of falling. I tried to cry out, but only a strained, hoarse sound escaped my lips. I felt my body lift up, and I jumped.

I looked up into Cameron's face as he was carrying me up the steps. I realized that I had been dreaming. The minor details of the dream already began to fade, but the major part – Grandma – stayed sharply in focus.

Still too tipsy to maintain total consciousness, I laid my head down on his strong shoulders and closed my eyes. He took a deep breath and sighed.

"Got me here carrying you like a baby. I don't know how you got drunk off that little bit of Bacardi..."

"Smirnoff," I slurred.

"Oh...Well, whatever it was, it's got you twisted. What am I supposed to do with you?" he asked tenderly.

Even with my eyes closed, I could tell he was turning the corner on the steps to the second floor. The shift in direction coupled with the small bouncy movements of him climbing the stairs made me feel a little more lightheaded.

"I know what you can do with me."

Then I slipped back into unconsciousness.

I awoke on his bed to the sound of a low, vibrating bass filling the room. The room was pitch-black, and the music blocked out any other sound. I had no idea where he was. Beyonce was talking to a distant lover in a breathy, husky voice; wearing his shirt to bed to fight off loneliness. If I ever needed it, this was definitely the song to get me in the mood. He could have easily skipped the rest of the playlist and left this song on repeat. Just the intro music alone made my panties damp.

Out of nowhere, I felt a hand touch my foot. I would have jumped had it not been for the alcohol slowing my reaction time. I could feel him move up my thighs towards the skirt. He put his hands on my hips and turned me on my stomach. Slipped my top over my head.

"Mmmm. What are you doing?" I asked as if I didn't know.

The clasp from my bra unhooked. He lifted my upper body to remove the bra and grazed my nipples in the process. I could feel the soft, pigmented flesh harden instantly. My skirt was the next item to exit.

Something warm dripped on my back. My mind clouded with alcohol, I pictured him above me, salivating over me.

Then, I remembered the massage oil.

The smell of almond and honey took over my senses. I couldn't tell whether the oil was getting warmer or if the heat was generating from my pores.

He straddled my legs and began to massage my back.

His hands are big. The palms alone, the

size of my face. In a steady motion, he massaged me back to full consciousness. His touch was firm and smooth. He moved down my back, over my small, shapely onion. His thumbs massaging dangerously close to the slit at the base.

He was teasing me again.

I shuddered with anticipation. A small moan escaped my lips. The combination of the almost X-rated massage and Destiny's Child was torture to my body. I badly wanted to feel him inside of me, but I tried to contain it. I learned by now that I couldn't rush him. All I could do was wait, as Michelle purred in the background.

Arousal became pressure starting at the tips of my toes. Desire was burning steam, rising within my body and scalding my insides on the way out. It threatened to make me scream with frustration. An ear-piercing, glass-shattering scream that would wake the neighbors.

Impatience had me squirming under his strong hands. I could feel tiny droplets of sweat erupt on my skin. The moment I thought my composure would break, he turned me over.

Cameron laid his solid, muscular frame on my tiny, soft body. The heat from skin overpowered my own. His body so large, it eclipsed me. I secretly loved how he made me feel so small just from the sheer size of him.

The thought momentarily disturbed me. Why did I want to feel like I was completely under his control? That I was totally defenseless. Utterly helpless. That notion left as quickly as it came once he put his full lips to mine.

His tongue was soft and warm.

And large.

Everything on him was.

Greedily, I took his tongue into my mouth

– eagerly awaiting him to enter another willing orifice. He pulled away and moved down to my neck. He gently kissed, sucked, and nipped at the sensitive area below my earlobe.

At one point, scared that he would go too far with his kisses, I tensed. After sensing my discomfort, he quickly left my neck, and I relaxed. I felt stupid for overreacting. Cameron knew not to put any marks on my body.

I started to worry that I had spoiled the mood. Just as doubt began to creep in and command my attention, soft wet heat glided over my nipples. Reflex and surprise caused me to moan aloud. The pleasure caught me off guard, and I couldn't hold back.

It was on now.

My defenseless whimpers caused him to react more aggressively. He picked up his pace of seduction and quickly kissed a path down my stomach, stopping briefly to dip his tongue in my navel. The sensation made me grab his head.

God, how I wished there was a little light at that moment. I could picture the moonlight illuminating his dark, mahogany skin. I wanted to see what he was about to do.

More so, I wanted him to see what he was about to do to me.

Roughly, he spread my legs wider. Thankfully, he bypassed his usual teasing trail down my thighs and went straight to the single source of my agony and pleasure.

Although the hair on my pubic area is short and nicely trimmed, my love below is bare. He found the small bud at the top and quickly flicked it with his tongue. I instantly lost what was left of my mind.

I relinquished all concepts of time.

Any concept of modesty or shame.

"Oh, God, Cameron! Oh..."

Breathing was a forgotten skill. I took in ragged, uneven gasps of air. The task was even more difficult with my mouth forcing out all kinds of nonsense. It was on autopilot. My mind was temporarily out of service. My body reacted on its own. My legs started to shake.

"Oh...Oh please...Please! Oh, God! Shit Cameron! Like that...Like...!"

His tongue skills brought me to climax quicker than I expected.

Colors exploded in the dark.

At that moment, I was seeing a deep crimson in the pitch black of the room. I came so hard, it felt as though my head would explode.

Cameron pulled his face up, the lower half of it soaked. I could almost hear the smile he made. I knew he loved every moment of it almost as much as I did. I know how much this turns him on.

As he pressed his weight on top of me, my body tensed once more. I braced myself not for the anticipation of pleasure, but of pain.

He was by far, the biggest man that I had ever slept with. I had only seen one other penis that large, and it was on a cheesy porno. My friends and I swore up and down that we would never let something that large even get close to our privates. If I had actually looked down that first night, he wouldn't have had a shot in hell to get me to try him. As his luck and my nervousness would have it, I never did look at the package before he wrapped it and delivered it priority mail. The shock from the pain of him entering me was so excruciating that I lost my breath. My nails instantly dug into his shoulders. I felt like I was being split in two – like it was my first time. Though it was painful, nothing about his technique was rough. He never pounded away that night. Very slow and sensual. It was just too big for my tiny frame. We both ended the night battered – his back and my poor kitty.

I remembered being so scared to have sex with him again. The only thing that got him a second chance was my pride. It wouldn't let me concede to a 24-year-old. I got into it a little quicker the second and subsequent times, but my body never got used to the first break. The moment that his huge dick penetrates my tight, little opening, stretching it to its limit, always causes a sharp, paralyzing pain to shoot through to my navel.

The muscles of my thighs tightened involuntarily, causing my body to slightly move up the bed as he pressed down trying to gain entry.

We've done this dance many times before.

"Relax, baby." He cooed softly in my ear.

"I know. I'm trying. It's just... Okay. Okay." The memory of the first night brought a new intensity of fear.

Against their will, I relaxed my thighs.

He slowly rubbed the massive tip against the outside, lubricating himself with my juices. Without warning, he entered me to full length.

A sharp gasp escaped before all air left my lungs. His hands cupped under my ass and lifted me slightly.

"Ohhhhh! Damn, girl! This pussy is so good!" He groaned in my ear – his face pressing into the side of my own.

I loved when he talked dirty to me, but I needed to get past that searing pain, first.

"*Focus*," I thought to myself.

I tried to control my breathing. Relax my muscles. I closed my eyes tighter and relaxed my thighs some more. Found his rhythm and mine. Warm pleasure crept up my body once more.

Before I completely lost it, I remembered something very important.

"B-Baby...Pl-Please...Don't cum... in me." I managed to stutter out.

"Wh-...Why, shit, why not?" He was having as difficult a time as I was communicating.

"Because...I...Oh, God!   Just because, please!"

I was tongue-tied. Couldn't get my mouth to cooperate with my brain. Couldn't get out that I had missed my pills for two days before I noticed – the stress of our long-term relationship was wearing on me. I couldn't risk getting pregnant now.

"Don't you want to feel me cum inside you?"

Why did he have to say it like that? I was on the brink of insanity. I had to wrap this up soon, while I still had some willpower.

"What about...oohhh...condom?"

We hadn't used those since we exchanged negative test results last winter.

"I need to feel you. All. Of. You." He stroked deep with each word to emphasize this.

"You're so warm...mmmm...So wet. Don't know if I...h-have anymore. I...I'll have to take it out. Get off the bed. Go looking for...some...have to stop."

He stroked deeper to prove his point. Aimed to the left. Held his weight on that spot for a few seconds. Made him stopping this sweet pain the last thing I wanted him to do.

End of discussion. I was past the point of

reason.

"Oh!   Okay!   Just.   Pull   out!   Please! I...I...!"

That   was   all   he   needed.   His   speed   increased.   More force in his stride.

"Is this the best dick you've ever had?"

"Yesss!"

My eyes rolled in the back of my head.

"This is my pussy, isn't it?"

"Uh huh! Yes! Please, yes!"

My nails raked his skin.

His   stroking   got   harder.   Turning   reward into   punishment.   Punishment   into   reward.   All kinds   of   pleading   words   escaped   my   lips.   This only   incited   him   further.   I   didn't   care.   I   wanted to be punished. Was willing to do hard time.

"Who   else   has   been   hitting   this   pussy   like this?"

"N-N-No one!"

"Who else makes you feel this good?"

"Nobody," I gasped.

"Do you love me?"

At   this   point,   I   could   have   promised   to   sell him   my   right   eye.   There's   not   much   I   wouldn't agree to in the throes of a pending orgasm. But there   was   no   need   to   answer   falsely   –no   matter how   unintentionally   –   to   this   question.   I   did   love him.

That was true to the very depth of my soul.

"Yes,"   I   said   weakly,   barely   able   to   gather air   enough   breathe.   Tears   slid   down   the   corners of my eyes.

"I love you too, Nia."

He   kissed   my   neck   hard   as   he   said   this. His   hands   reached   down   and   grabbed   my   legs. They   were   forced   back   behind   my   head   –   pinned under   his   massive   shoulders.   With   my   body completely under his control, he began to pound into my nadir.

Not a maddening, hyper, irregular speed that most young guys have when they think they're actually doing something. Trying to "beat the pussy up" as they call it. It was a steady, controlled, and calculated beat meant to send me over the edge.

Oh my God! The pain! It threatened to make me scream bloody murder. *"But sweet Jesus! The pleasure!"*

I couldn't take it anymore. I didn't know whether to push him off me or hold on for dear life. I chose the latter and dug my nails into his back. I could feel him getting harder. The head swelling.

I couldn't breathe. Panic crept in as I lost control over my body. I didn't know what was happening. Cold sweat broke out of my pores. My own heartbeat thudded in my ear. The sound, drowning out all others. Felt as if I was dying from pure ecstasy. My hearing was fading and for a split second, all I could hear was a humming sound. Just when I thought I really was going to die – or at least pass out – it came.

Waves and waves and waves of draining pleasure washed over me. My body convulsed so violently that I would have been scared, had I any rational thought left. My breath came back and with each wave, I let out a dragging moan. I couldn't stop. I saw red behind closed eyelids. Felt heaven between clenched thighs.

After what seemed like an eternity, the waves started to ebb into tiny ripples. My heart, pounding violently in my chest moments before, began the process to resume its normal rhythm. I almost slipped into post-coital unconsciousness

– except...

I could feel a pulsating contraction within me, but it wasn't coming from me.

"*Is he...Did he...?*" I thought to myself, not fully able to grasp what was happening at that moment.

I'm not sure how my brain singled out that one sensation out of many, but it did. At his size, it was hard not to feel even the slightest movement when he was inside of me. And though he pulled out, motioned like he was going in his hand, and quickly left for the bathroom, I already knew it. He came in me.

As if I didn't believe what I'd just felt, I slowly moved my hand down to my sore area and inserted a finger halfway in. I brought it back up to my nose and sniffed.

Definitely, semen.

The toilet flushed.

I began to see a soft haze of red again in space of his room, but this one was different. It was born out of anger.

"Mmmm. That was too good, baby." He crawled into bed, put his arm around my waist and kissed my cheek. "You really wore me out. I wanted you so bad today. You just don't know. When you were sitting there in that skirt...What's wrong?"

I was sitting up with my knees to my chest and my arms wrapped around them. My posture never changed when he got into bed. Not when he put his hands on my body. Not when he kissed me. It was dark in the room, but he didn't need light to tell that I was upset. I was almost shaking with anger.

"The fuck did you just do?" Tears were beginning to form in my eyes.

"Uh…What are you…?"

"You came in me!"

"Wha—? No, no, I pulled out. That's why I went to the bathroom right away to wash…"

"You. Came. In. Me." I said getting out of the bed. "I felt it. And there's semen in me! Don't lie! I know!" Pain as I stubbed my toe on the dresser trying to find the light switch. I ignored it. My hand grazed the wall until I found what I needed. The brightness temporarily hurt my eyes as the pupils tried to adjust and constrict.

"Well, okay, I didn't get all of it, but I didn't purposefully…I haven't done that in so long, baby. I slipped up. My bad!" He said apologetically with a smile. "Why did you even make me…?"

"I messed up on my pills."

I stopped searching for my clothes to look at him when I said this. The realization sunk in. His smile was gone.

"Why…Why didn't you just tell me?"

"I couldn't get the words out in time. You were…Does it even matter? If I told you that I didn't want you to come in me, it doesn't matter what the reason was. It's my body!"

Who the hell did he think he was? I scrambled around the room looking for my clothes.

"I would have been extra careful. I got caught up in the moment. You know what you do to me…Babygirl, why are you overreacting like this? You know I wouldn't put you at risk on purpose. I said I'm sorry."

He kept his voice was soft and low. I knew he was sorry. Cameron wasn't a man who liked to plead with anybody, but here he was trying. I could see the emotion in his eyes. He was scared that I was going to leave.

Still, I couldn't let it go.

"No, actually you didn't say you were sorry! You said 'My bad'!" What the hell is that? You didn't accidentally spill water on me! You could have gotten me pregnant! At least we agree on one thing. You are one sorry…"

The vibrating noise stopped my insult mid-air. It was coming from the floor near my over-turned purse. The contents had spilled out and my phone lay right next to Cameron's foot. He picked it up, looked at the number, and then looked at me. He held the phone in front of him a little longer than needed, as if contemplating taking action, before handing it to me. From the look he gave me, I knew he recognized the number. Instantly, my heart started to race. I could feel my stomach bottom out. It was three-something in the morning. The phone stopped ringing before I could see the number on the screen – leaving behind the missed-call symbol. Before I had a chance to check the menu, the vibrating started right back up.

It was James. He was calling from my house.

The look on my face changed from anger to fear.

The look on Cameron's face changed from fear to anger.

"I thought he was going to be gone all weekend?" Voice still low, but now menacing. His Asian-like eyes narrowed even further.

"Thought he was, too," I said in an anxious voice. I quickly scanned the room for my possessions. Five minutes ago, I was only pretending to want to leave. Now, it was all I could do not to run out the house half-dressed. Panic screamed in my brain.   I was concentrating hard not to rush my movements too much. I had to deal with James, but I didn't want Cameron to know how scared I was.   I didn't want to upset him even more. I still cared about his feelings.

"Why don't you just answer the phone?"

And he was still a cop.

His police tactics kicked in. He was toying with me. Trying to unnerve me. Make me slip up in some way, for some reason: anger, hurt, maybe. I didn't know. Maybe he wanted to make me mess things up with James. He knew I couldn't talk to James with him standing in front of me. Staring directly at me. I wasn't a good liar and that would only make it worse. I was too nervous right now, and he wasn't helping.

"I'll call him when I get in the car."

"No, why don't you call him now. Waiting will just make him even more suspicious."

Police tactics, again.

I stared at his serious, handsome face and frowned. This reverse psychology was beginning to irritate me. He must have recognized that look because his tone changed.

"I thought you were staying the weekend – or at least the night." The look on his face softened. He really didn't want me to leave.

The sad part is that neither did I. I wanted to spend the night with him a lot more than I should have. Each time we met, it became harder and harder to leave him. I wished he knew this. I wished he knew that I didn't want to leave – but, for James' sake, I had to go. I wished he could understand how I could feel love and need for one person, while still feeling love and obligation for another. I wished he knew it was possible to be in love with two people, at the same time, but in different ways.

I wish he knew how the look in his eyes of anger, dissolving into sadness was slowing my racing heartbeat – weighing it down with a painful, ache. Wished he knew that those tears forming in my eyes were not from the fear of James finding out, but from the thought of hurting Cameron. They were from the thought of leaving Cameron. Of not knowing when we'd be able to spend this much time together. I was missing him already.

"You know I can't stay now. Besides, after what happened tonight, I don't know if I would stay if I could." I wanted to sound angry. I was trying to turn it around and make it seem like he was the main reason I was leaving. It wasn't working.

The phone went off again. I couldn't find my other shoe. Anxiety was creeping up my spine. I had to end this conversation as quickly as possible.

"Look, I know you can't stay. Just go home, take care of what you need to take care of, and call me tomorrow to let me know you're okay. We'll make this up another time." He started scanning the room for my other shoe.

"I don't think...Maybe there shouldn't be another time." He stopped searching through discarded clothing and looked at me. "We shouldn't be doing this. I...I don't know what I was thinking getting us into this."

He looked at me, but his expression remained the same. "Look, don't say that. You're just tired and stressed out right now. Go home and get some sleep. We'll talk more about this later."

I found my other sandal and slipped it on.

I sat on the edge of the bed and stared at my feet for a few seconds – lost for words. I didn't know what to say before leaving, but I didn't want to leave without saying anything.

Basically, I didn't want to leave.

The vibrating phone interrupted my silent reflection and made me look in his direction. He had never bothered to put his boxers on. Those dark eyes held not one glimpse of self-consciousness. I glanced over his naked perfection once more before I stood up and walked towards him.

I reached up on the very tip of my toes. Slipped my arms around his neck as he leaned down towards me in response. We kissed softly. Slowly. Mouths slightly open. Just the tips of our tongues touched, separated, and touched again. So much feeling in that kiss.

I pulled away slowly, looked up into his somber face, unable to hold back the tears any longer, and whispered, "I'm sorry."

I turned around before he could respond and left out of the room, down the stairs, and out the front door – closing it softly behind me. I couldn't look back.

Now, I'm trying to decide what I'm going to tell James. Why did he even come back early? I hope it's not an emergency, because I can't talk to him right now. And, why did he have to go to my house? Why couldn't he just leave me a message, assume I was sleeping—like most people do at 3 am—and call me back in the morning? What could I say to him? I had no clue how to explain where I've been at this time of night.

Who could give me an alibi? Taz? What if he already called her? I didn't give her a pre-fab excuse, because I didn't think I needed to. James wasn't supposed to be back until Monday. Nope. If he called her looking for me, she would have been calling me as much as James.

He doesn't know Jaz's number. Thank goodness, they're not very buddy-buddy. I could use her as an excuse.

"Damn!"

He *is* buddy-buddy with Curtis—her so-called man—and he's there with her this week. He and James know each other from school, and they always get real chummy when we all get together. James might mention something about tonight and homeboy will look at him like he's crazy. That's all I need.

And there's no way I could ever let Curtis know any of this and expect him to keep it a secret. We tolerate each other, but I know he feels the same way about me as I do about him – no love lost. Curtis would love to open the lid to my can of worms as many times as I've tried to blow up his spot. He's a worthless, cheating asshole, and he knows I know this. I just wish Jasmine would see it, because I stopped trying to tell her a long time ago.

Plan B, out of the question.

What if he called my mom's house? I didn't want to worry her this time of night if he hadn't called her. I really didn't want to tell her anything if I don't have to. She loves James – right down to his dirty drawers. If I told her, she might just sell me out under the guise of doing "the right thing."

Definitely wasn't calling mom. Taz was my only option if he hadn't gotten to her already.

The screen light flashed again.

I looked down to see if Taz was calling me,

maybe worried about me. Maybe trying to warn me.

It was Cameron.

I didn't want to talk to him at that moment. Too many things on my mind. Tears were forming again. I was going to have to figure out how to stay away from him. I couldn't keep doing this.

Just as I looked up from the phone, I noticed something in the middle of the parkway trying to cross the road. My eyes widened in horror as I saw a little girl with two long ponytails on the side of her head, looking directly at me. Confused, I put my foot on the brakes and blinked away the tears. My vision cleared in a fraction of a second, and to my relief, I realized it was just a dog – a cocker spaniel.

Still trying to avoid hitting it, I put on the brakes and turned my wheel sharply to the left. Too sharply. The car began tail-spinning. I closed my eyes and prayed. *"Please God, take care of everybody."*

I could feel myself spinning, but it felt like it was in slow motion. At that moment, I knew that was it. This had to be the end. The screeching of the tires was going to be the last thing I heard.

All of a sudden, all movement stopped. I couldn't hear anything. Not even my own breathing. I was too scared to breathe. Too scared to open my eyes. I knew the next thing I would see would be the lights on the ceiling at the county's Shock Trauma unit. A masked surgeon above me, telling me to hold on as they wheeled me into the OR. I was even more afraid I'd see the bene-volent eyes of The Son of God, himself.

I opened one eye and looked at the dashboard of the car. I opened the other eye and focused two visions into one. I scanned the view from the windshield. It was still foggy. Still night. Still the B-W parkway, except that I was looking at it from the grass median, facing the opposite direction.

Tears filled my eyes again, but these came from pure relief. I couldn't believe I was on 295, at now four in the morning, facing northbound on the southbound side. The humor of it all got to me. Even though I should have been busting a 3-point turn to get in the right direction before Park Police made their rounds, I started to giggle. This giggle turned into a full-blown belly-busting, sidesplitting laughter.

Typical.

How did I, Niani Jones, get myself into another predicament? At least this time, I didn't have to call my cousin from the back of a closet, in the locked bedroom of someone's house that I didn't know, to come get me out of this mess. The thought of Taz and I somewhere in Southeast, crouching on the floor of someone's closet and holding on to each other for dear life—while a major fight was going on outside—was making me laugh even harder. While our parents thought we were safe at school, we were there thinking that we were about to die.

But we got out of there okay.

I'll get out of this situation, as usual.

The laughter died down as I tried to catch my breath.

The phone flashed again in a silent ring.

I looked at my phone, then back out through the windshield. Something off to the left caught my eye. It was barely in the beam of the headlights, but I could just make it out.

It was the dog.

Its head, front legs, and upper body were facing me, but its lower half was twisted horribly in the opposite direction – mangled beyond recognition. Eyes stared blankly at me as it struggled to take in air. Mouth open. Tongue hanging on the ground. Blood trickling from it. Its chest moved in an offbeat, seesaw motion – one-half going up as the other half went down. The look of shock in its eyes as its body fought to keep functioning.

After what seemed like an eternity, it took one short gasp in and a much longer breath out.

There was no more movement.

Its dead, fixed eyes looked directly at me. Accusing me.

Condemning me.

My phone angrily lit in the dark.

What was left of my emotional sanity cracked into a million pieces.

"Love is like a drug. It costs too much, it fucks with your mind, and it only feels good for the first fifteen minutes."
Jaz

Chapter 2:
Jasmine

I've got twenty minutes left of my workout. Twenty minutes more of intense physical pain. Twenty minutes more, and I can stop obsessing over my problems until the next workout.

Honestly, the word "problems" is misleading. I only have one problem at this moment. The same problem I've had for the last 9 years. The same problem that has been the root of most of my issues for the last eight years. The same problem that I have been trying to solve through mental workouts I take during my physical workouts.

The same problem I picture myself having when I'm eighty years old, living alone with no children and about four cats.

Curtis.

The thought of his name made me pick up my pace on the elliptical. I turned my headphones up and zoned out on the rock song blasting from my IPod. It was Puddle of Mudd . The lead singer screaming his pain to the woman who rejected him. Trying to convince her that his love is the best thing for her.

This song reminded me of him —of us— so much. Nowadays, most songs seem to remind me of him in some way or another.

My two shameful loves: Curtis and rock music. At least the latter brings me more joy than pain.

My choice of music has been a source of ridicule amongst my close friends for some time now. My love of alternative rock/pop started in the eighty's as a little child when there were no hip/hop-only radio stations in Maryland. The most popular stations played hits from all genres. From LL Cool J to Madonna. New Edition to U2. Michael Jackson to Michael Jackson.

In my teens, with the rising popularity of rap and hip/hop, my love for rock music inversely died down.   WPGC, WKYS, 92Q, even Flavor 1580. There were so many hip/hop stations and so many songs to listen to; there was no room for any alternative.

From the politically-conscience lyrics of Public Enemy and KRS1 to the socially irrespons- ible lyrics of NWA and 2LiveCrew. And of course, there were the songs from others like Busta Rhymes, Jay-Z, and Biggie, that ran from one end of that spectrum to the other. The afrocentric- ness of DeLa Soul. The hormone-charged freaki- ness of R-Kelly. The scary intensity of Tupac. The laid-back pimp-soul of Snoop. The strong, feminine, sexual independence of Aaliyah and TLC. The raunchy, bold, sexual independence of Lil' Kim and Foxy. The lighthearted, consistent fun of A Tribe Called Quest and the deep, pro- phetic flow of Naz. All other types of music were put to the back burner.

My love of alternative music was rekindled

somewhere during the mid-nineties, sparked by accident, watching MTV. I saw Nirvana's "Smell Like Teen Spirit" video. The dark, unfocused scenes of teenagers in various outfits, in various stages of high school activities coupled with Kurt Kobain's tortured voice and haunted expression caught my eye for a second. It was just enough time for the hypnotic melody of the guitar to draw me into Nirvana's version of teen unrest. By the time the hard-hitting chorus took over and transformed everyone from depressed, lethargic zombies to energy-filled symbols of rebellion and expression, I was hooked. After that awakening, I continued to add various artists to my secret stockpile of rock music.

Hip/hop was and is always will be my true love. I just stray from her pleasures every once in awhile. Usually, it's an awards show performance, or an advertisement, or a movie soundtrack that introduces me to artists like Coldplay, or The Fray, or even Lady Gaga. My secret love interest is new, exciting in the same way, but different.

Hip/Hop centers around the beat. The beat makes and breaks the song. It comes on strong and leads with confidence.

Rock focuses on the melody. The beat usually follows, sometimes switching pace to keep up or slow down. With rock, the melody is first violin, and the beat is second fiddle.

Hip/Hop is about action. It causes you to get up, to move, to take control. Rock causes you to stop and reflect. Sometimes open wounds. Sometimes heals them.

Hip/hop is direct, in-your-face, no-holds-barred. Rock is usually, alternate meanings, hidden agendas. Both exciting. Both different.

The chorus of the song was coming in hard. The lead went from mournful singing to yelling at the top of his lungs. Giving me a boost of energy. Making me sweat. Making me think.

I was moving like a mad woman. Trying to make my legs move fast enough to carry me past my worries. Walk on troubled waters.

Sweat rolled down my forehead. Into my eyes. Stinging them. I wiped away and pretended it was only the sweat I was clearing away. I was getting angry. Angry at him. Angry at myself. Wished I could just erase the memory of him for good.

The song ended and moved to the next track. One of my favorites of all time. Bonnie Raitt's "I can't make you love me."

Oh yes, I like me a little country, too.

This song was my signal. Not only to slow down my workout to a cool down speed, but also to remember. I leave this song as the last thought on my mind as I end my mental workout. Maybe if I hear it enough times, my heart will believe it. Fall in agreement with what my mind realized awhile ago.

I can't make Curt love me. At least not the way I need him to.

"I'll close my eyes, and then I won't see
A love you don't feel, when you're holding me.
Morning will come, and I'll do what's right
Just give me 'til then, to give up this fight..."

The reality of her words cuts me every time. I feel like she wrote that song for me. Probably for every woman at some time in their lives. I feel a lump in my throat as the reality sinks in deeper. I slowed down not because I needed to, but because I had to. My poor heart is breaking again, and it just can't keep up with the demands of my body right now. I let the sweat run into my eyes this time because it's camouflaging tears.

"I can't make you love me if you don't.
You can't make your heart feel something it won't.
Here in the dark. In these final hours,
I will lay down my heart, and I'll feel the power,
> *But you won't,*
> *No you won't..."*

I put the towel to my face and held it, let it absorb the salty solution of sweat and tears. Held it there until my breathing slowed with the rhythm of my heart.

"Fuck love!"

I hated feeling like this. Like someone else. Not myself.

All because of love.

Love is like a drug. It costs too much, it fucks with your mind, and it only feels good for the first fifteen minutes.

The pain throbbed away, and I composed myself.

I looked at my reflection in the wall mirror and wondered for a second what was wrong with me. I knew that I was a good-looking woman. It was evident in the stares, the smiles, and the propositions that I got on the regular. I looked at the sheen of sweat glistening off of my caramel-brown skin and beamed with pride. Despite everything I hated about my body, I loved my skin.

I just hated that some people were so narrow-minded when it came to skin color.

It amazed me how the lighter tones had so

many distinctions between them (red-bone, light-skinned, yellow, high-yellow, etc), but if you were brown-skinned or dark-skinned, you were grouped into one.

There were so many beautiful shades of brown, but some people don't acknowledge that. There was caramel, cinnamon, pecan, almond, cocoa, honey, mahogany, chocolate, dark chocolate, ebony, and so on.

And so many different undertones to go with these browns: red, yellow, blue...So many varieties.

I glanced over my skin once more.

I loved my medium-brown skin. In an area with a majority Black population, it never gave me any problems. It wasn't light enough to be hated. It wasn't dark enough to be teased. It was neutral. It was beautiful. Smooth and clear. Red undertones complimented with jet-black hair. Gifts from my African ancestry mixed with Native American blood.

I continued to look in the mirror, but this time, the negatives came into focus.

My forehead was too big. Mouth to narrow for my full-lips. Eyes too slanted. Jaw too square. Short neck. Short legs. Not enough cleavage. Not enough ass.

At 5'5" and 147 lbs, I could probably lose a few more pounds. I have a naturally muscular build, but from genetics, not because I wanted it. It keeps me in a size 8 easily, without too much effort, but I have to make sure I don't start looking like the wrestler Chyna.

I wished I were softer.
Curvier.
Perfect.
"Then maybe..."

I had to stop those kinds of thoughts as soon as they entered my mind. I know there's nothing wrong with me. It was Curtis.

Or better yet, it was me allowing Curtis to treat me the way he does.

The guy in the mirror distracted me from my self-evaluation. He was looking right at me. Running on the treadmill. Not breaking eye contact. He was a White guy. Cute. Very nice body. Dark hair with the palest blue eyes I have ever seen. He had some color. Italian, maybe, or just a tan.

He smiled.

I smiled back. My heart wasn't in it.

However cute he was, I couldn't return the interest he was showing.

All of my interests in men lie with Curt. I just couldn't find any real desire for any other man, but him. He had my heart and soul.

He was eating me, slowly, painfully, from the inside out.

Consuming me like cancer.

Living off everything I had to give while returning nothing.

I had to find the courage to let go, but I didn't know how. I wasn't sure I wanted to. Because then, I would have to be alone to face myself. At least I knew what to expect from him, although, unfortunately, that wasn't very much.

What I didn't know was what to expect from myself.

Fear of the unknown had me paralyzed.

I looked away from the guy, and then back. He was still smiling.

So was I.

I thought about going over to him. Introducing myself. Starting a small conversation.

Exchanging numbers.

Taking a step away from my addiction.

Instead, I stepped off the treadmill, walked behind him, and left the Sport Fit without looking in his direction.

"She was my best friend...I envied her."
Taz

Chapter 3:
Tazanna

Another day, another dollar. Another STD.
Another teen pregnancy.

I usually say this mantra to myself when
I'm getting frustrated. Or overwhelmed. Or angry. Or just plain bored.

I say this a lot when I'm working in the office.

Some days, when it's really bad — when I
want to scream at the top of my lungs – I'll mum-
ble it out loud. The staff knows this is a sign that
I'm reaching my limit. Most of the time, they stay
out of my way and make sure everything else is
running smoothly. Sometimes they chant it with
me. All to let me know we're in this together.

I mumbled my mantra while looking under
the microscope; praying that I'd only see signs of
a simple vaginal infection. Not some sexually
transmitted disease. From her symptoms, I was
expecting to see tiny trichomonad swimming
around in the sample of fluid from her vagina.

The only thing I saw moving was even tini-
er sperm.

"Yuck!" I wish these girls would stop hav-

ing unprotected sex. At least stop having it before they came to see me.

I reviewed the chart again before I walked
into the exam room.

Tonesha Settles.   14 years old. One previous abortion.   History of chlamydia (once last
summer and again this past April), trichomonas,
bacterial vaginosis, HPV, abnormal pap smear,
and marijuana use. A former preemie baby, born
at 28 weeks to a cocaine-positive mom.   Lives
with her aunt over in Landover Hills.   Three sex
partners since her start of sexual activity 2 years
ago.

14 years old.

At least she's on birth control.

I knocked on the door and went in.
Tonesha was still on the exam table nervously
playing with her airbrushed, acrylic nails.

"I told you that you could get dressed.
We're done with the exam."

"Sorry.   My mind was wandering.   Guess
I'm a little nervous."

"Well, so far, so good.   It looks like you only have bacterial vaginosis – again.   As you know,
it's a harmless vaginal infection.   Not sexually
transmitted.   Once the cultures come back, I'll let
you know the results."

"Well then how come this is the 3rd time?
You sure my boyfriend doesn't need to be treated
this time?"

"Well, current studies show no benefit to
treating male partners for BV.   They say it's not
passed on sexually, but a few of my colleagues
have this theory.   Dr. Michaels calls it Double D
Syndrome."

"What's that?'

"Dirty Dick Syndrome.   We find that if a

woman or her partner is not being monogamous, a lot of times she ends up having female problems – namely frequent yeast or bacterial infections. Only noticed in the clinical setting. It hasn't been proven, but like one of my friends told me 'If your man's messing around, something's always going wrong down there.' Are you monogamous?"

"Oh yeah! I only like men."

Without thinking, I laughed. She looked at me a little confused.

"No, no, I mean are you being faithful?"

"Of course!   I can't be sleepin' with a bunch of men."

"What about your boyfriend?"

"Well, I don't know, I think Tron is sleepin' with his babymama again."

"Tron? As in Voltron?"

"You so funny, Dr. K. His full name is De'Antron."

"*Even worse,*" I thought.   She said his name ("De-Aan-Tron") like I was supposed to be impressed.   The names people give their kids. There ought to be a law.

"Anyway, Tron be saying he need to go over there to help her with the baby 'cause she tired or something. And he don't be answering my pages at night."

"*People still have pagers? Who's providing service to them?*"

"And you know she's pregnant again, but he swears it's not by him."

"Well, what do you think, Ms. Settles?" I called her Ms. Settles on purpose. Even though she's young enough to be my child—if I had her around her age—I wanted her to remind her to be responsible. If she's going to engage in adult activities, she needs to start thinking and acting like an adult.

"I think he's cheating."

"Good. At least I didn't have to tell you the obvious." I really didn't mean to sound sarcastic. It amazes me, the stories some girls and women will believe. "So are you using protection?"

"Yup."

"Come on Monesha." I already knew the answer. I saw the sperm. I just wanted her to think she couldn't get anything past me. Also, I wanted her to know she could tell me the truth and not be ashamed.

"Well, not all the time. Not really anymore."

"Sweetie, you have to get in the habit of using condoms all the time. You're protected from another pregnancy, but you leave yourself wide open for anything else – including HIV. You've been lucky so far. What if you get something you can't get rid of like herpes, warts, or HIV?"

She nodded. Concern shadowed her face as the seriousness of it all started to sink in.

"I don't want to lecture you, but I am trying to scare you. With good reason. Do you know last week I had to tell a 16-year-old that she was HIV positive? She had only been with two partners in her life. She had been having sex less than you. Is any of this worth it?"

"Damn! Sixteen years old?"

"Yup."

Suddenly, the reality of it all sunk in, and she stared at me in amazement.

"You still want to go to college? Become a teacher?"

"Yeah."

"How are you going to teach kids if you

can't learn yourself?"

"Your right, Dr. K. From now on, I'm using condoms all the time. I can take some with me right?"

"Take as many as you want. Get more whenever you need it."

"What I need to do is leave Tron's ass alone. Why he gotta have some bomb-ass dick, though."

"Having good dick isn't everything. It's not much really. Where does his babymama live?"

"In the projects. Some ghetto-ass, run-down apartment in Barry Farms."

"Does he give her any money?"

"No. He not working. She get welfare and section 8. I think he's fuckin'—um, excuse me—screwing her so he can have a place to stay, since his grandma kicked him out. He wanted to stay with me, but you know my auntie ain't having that."

"Hmmm, broke and living in someone else's house. He sounds like a real catch. What good is dick when you're homeless or hungry? You damn sure can't eat it."

"Knowin' Tron's ass, I wouldn't want to."

We both laughed

I needed that.

I hoped I had gotten through to her, at least somewhat. I was tired of seeing the same faces over again for the same reasons.

Each time they came in, the light in their future dimmed more and more.

"We're running low on Depo shots. When does the next shipment come in? Oh, and I thought I was supposed to be off the 8th of next month."

My nurse Yvette was bombarding me with questions that I had no answers to. Why did Nia have to take off today of all days? This place is a madhouse. I really need my office manager.

"You'll have to talk to Niani about that tomorrow. She'll be in. As long as we have enough Depo shots for today, I'm good. We'll deal with tomorrow when tomorrow comes."

"Is she okay? You know, I dreamt of fish last night. She's not pregnant is she?"

"God, I hope not!"

"No. She got into a little car accident over the weekend. She was kind of frazzled...."

"Oh my God! Is she okay?"

"Yeah. She just hit a dog. You know how she is about animals. She was just a little upset."

Actually, she was hysterical—babbling about James, and Cameron, and seeing her dead grandmother—when she called. I thought maybe James found out and beat her so bad, he knocked something loose. I was up searching for my clothes and ready to go get her, when she starting screaming, "She's dead! I tried to stop! I tried to stop!"

That made me stop dead in my tracks. I wasn't sure what had happened at that point, but I was thinking if a crime was committed, I didn't think I could help her get out of this one.

I finally got her to tell me what happened that night. I was trying to get her to calm down and help think up a story for James when she suddenly stopped crying. Her breathing normalized and she started speaking in a calm, emotionless voice.

(This scared me even more.)

She assured me that she knew what to tell James: That she couldn't sleep and she went to the office to work on some chart audits. I was to verify that, if James called me—which he never did, thank God. She was going to bury the dog (This really creeped me out.) and take her car in Monday to get it cleaned and serviced. She told me was okay. Just a little upset, but she would get herself together. I insisted on meeting her to make sure she was all right, but she told me not to come. ("Terrence would be up soon and I don't want to get him involved.")

My husband Terrence always got up around the crack of dawn. He was a perpetual morning person, but thank goodness, he slept like a log. He didn't even stir while I was whispering to Nia on the phone right next to him. (I don't know how many times I've sneaked out of the house at night to return with him in the same exact position hours later.)

Despite her reassurance, something was bothering me. The way she shut everything off and began talking calmly, as if nothing was wrong, made me uneasy. She made a good argument, though, and I was so tired, I let it go – as long as she promised to call in the morning as soon as things settled.

At least I convinced her not bury that dog.

This was just one of the many stressful (and sometimes bizarre) situations that came with being the best friend of Niani Jones.

Growing up as Nia's friend was far from uneventful. She's put me in countless uncomfortable, embarrassing, and sometimes, even dangerous positions over the years. Nia was always so headstrong and outgoing. She had so many friends. So many admirers. People thought I tagged along because of that. Even my parents thought I was just being a follower.

But I saw what others didn't. She was impulsive. She was too trusting. Too naive. She had a lot of book smarts, but was lacking in the commonsense department. She loved excitement too much. She loved attention too much. And she definitely loved men too much. She lived for the moment and never thought things through.

I was such a quiet, easygoing child. Always wanting to be the peacemaker. Always willing to sacrifice for harmony. The opposite of Nia, people mistook my quiet nature for a shy spirit. My reserved attitude for a timid personality. My passiveness for weakness.

I followed her into some risky situations or got involved when she needed my help, not because I was a follower, but because I wanted to protect her. I know I'm the reason she didn't lose her virginity in the 10th grade to that senior who was sleeping with half of the girls (and probably a quarter of the boys) in high school. When she didn't notice a foreign smell polluting the familiar scent of marijuana, I was the one who kept her from smoking Love Boat—weed mixed with PCP. I've even kept her from being date-raped—twice. The last one, I thought we were both going to be statistics.

Without someone to look over her and watch her back, she wouldn't have gotten as far as she has. She could have been just like some of these girls that come into my office, throwing their lives away for some worthless boy.

My parents had a love-hate relationship with her. They loved how she took me under her wing socially. She made me lift my nose out of my books from time to time – made me peak my head out of my shell. She would always include me in every outing. Never let anyone talk about me. She's even got into a couple of fights over me. Made me take an interest in myself, my looks, my clothes. Made me popular by default. My parents loved this the most. Popularity was something that my parents –both doctors, both bookworms, and both social outcasts – never had themselves. It was a dream for them to be smart and popular. It was a dream made reality, thanks to Nia.

It was never something I was concerned about.

I could always see the bigger picture. I pictured the lives that some of those oh-so-fly, popular girls, who were so caught up in having the latest Louis Vuitton bag, and the latest Versace jeans, and the hottest, drug-dealing boyfriend, instead of their schoolwork, would have in the future. I could picture some of them ending up in my office; coming in for care, pregnancy after pregnancy. (One of those girls actually did.)

I wasn't comfortable with the attention that came with being known in school. Before Nia, I had never thought I was attractive. Always too tall for my age, I maxed out at 5'10" in the 8th grade. My skin was too light. My features too European. If it weren't for my dirty-blond hair being so kinky, no one would have known that I was black.

My great-aunt, a color-struck, mean-spirited, old woman so pale, her cat-like eyes were golden-yellow, once told me I was color-wasted. She said to me, as she fingered my hair with pity, unconscious of her own self-hatred, that she didn't know how someone as pretty and as light as me "with them hazel eyes and that small pointy nose" could have hair so nappy.

"It look like blonde steel wool. Feel like,

too."

She blamed my dad for this transgression. In addition to not being a Proctor, he had the nerve to be darker than the color of a paper bag.

If I wasn't being teased in school for my height ("Hey, Shaq!", "Andrea the Giant!"), or my complexion ("Ay, White gurl, let me borrow a pencil.", "You okay, Snowflake?"), I was being teased for my hair ("Buck White", "Whoopi"). My mother, who never had to so much as press her fine, wavy hair, did not believe in perms. Unfortunately for me, she also didn't know how to do kinky hair. It was either in two unevenly parted Afro puffs—the sides and the kitchen a matted mess—or a bush with a bow on the side.

The only time it looked nice was when Aunt Tanya, (Dad's side, of course) would cornrow or press it for me. Or if a classmate took pity on me and braided my hair at recess. They would be amazed at the familiar, coarse texture coming from my exotically colored hair. I always enjoy these moments, reveling in the mutual conformation of my blackness.

My mom finally consented to let my hair get relaxed in the 8th grade – at Nia's persistent requests. Our first attempt was with a mild kiddie perm that Nia used when she used to perm her hair. It barely made a dent in the resistant kinks of my strong, thick hair. We learned our lesson and used Mizani super strength the next time with good results.

"You look like Vanessa Williams, with no butt and hardly any lips." She told me after she combed my hair out of the wrap.

I loved my hair, but the new look and better sense of style got me more unwanted attention – from horny boys and hating girls. Nia had gotten into a couple of people's faces over someone thinking that I wanted their scraggly little boyfriend, who couldn't help but stare in their presence.

Like I said, my parents loved the status that being Nia's best friend brought. But they hated the situations that seemed to happen only when she was around. If only they knew the half of them, they would have banned both of us from even speaking on the phone. They knew she was a sweet girl, but they felt she could be a negative influence on me. They never understand that I was trying to be a positive influence on her.

She was my best friend, and I loved her like a sister. I pitied her. I envied her.

I felt sorry that it seemed like she had it all going for her, but that she had issues deeper than even she could see.

I envied the fact that she could live in the moment and not be crippled by the "what if's." Not be scared to act. I sometimes resented that she would do whatever she wanted, without considering the consequences, and then could call on someone, namely me, for help when things got bad. I hated the fact that without much thought, effort, or planning, she seemed to have everything handed to her on a silver platter – her looks, her boyfriends, her friends, and her career.

Sometimes, I wanted her to fall flat on her face. If only to prove to her and the universe that you can't live life so carelessly and still get away with it.

Sometimes, I wanted to be just like her.

This is the nature of our friendship.

My parents weren't the only ones who had a love-hate relationship with Niani.

"Are you listening to me?"

Yvette broke me out of my trance.

"What did you say?"

"I said to have her call me to make sure she's okay."

"I will. Sorry about that. I was just think-ing about the hospital. I have to make rounds when I leave here."

"You're always thinking about work. Too young to be so caught up in your career. You need to get away sometimes. Take a break. So, we still on for lunch after work Friday?"

Every other Friday is my early day. The office closes at 12:30.

"Yup. Jasper's again. Just don't drink like you did last time. I really don't feel like driving you home again."

"Gurrl, those two Bone Crushers had me twisted! Don't worry, though. I don't drink like that during the daytime."

"Yeah, you know Mr. Yvette will kick your ass if you show up drunk at two in the after-noon."

"He'll try, but he'll lose!" She laughed.

"Let me go see this last patient so we can all get out of here. Tell Maria she can clean and sterilize all of the specs now. I won't be using an-ymore."

Maria was our medical assistant. She was from El Salvador, young, hard-working, and she doubled as a translator for my Hispanic patients. All my Spanish words came in French.

"Oooo! Here he comes, y'all!"

Keisha, my ghetto-fab receptionist, yelled down the hall. She popped her head around the corner, long, hand-decorated gel-wrapped nails gripping the doorframe. The curls from her half-wig (or swig as she calls it) bouncing along with her excited gestures.

She must have been talking about the lab pick-up guy, Eric. "Irk," (as Keisha pronounces it in her typical D.C accent) came by every day at 5pm to pick up office specimens and deliver them to Lab, Inc. Not the most professional guy around, he was friendly and, at least he had a job – though I'm not sure how, since he seemed as dumb as a doorknob.

Despite his ignorance, he was one of the finest men I've ever laid eyes on. Caramel-brown skin. Tattoos on his arms, chest, and back. Curly, black hair done in impeccable, elaborate cornrows. A new style every week. You just know some chickenhead is doing his hair for free just to be able to get that close to him. Neatly trimmed mustache and goatee. Full lips. Thick eyebrows. One of them was pierced. (This made me a little nervous about his sexual preference. Too many men on the down-low in this area for my liking.) He was a pretty-boy thug. Soft features, rough edge. A little on the short side and a little too young for my tastes. Still, he was very nice to look at.

Keisha ran back to her seat and tried to look like she was busy as Eric stepped through the door. He strutted to the front desk and smiled.

"Hey, Keish. Got any labs for me."

"Hey, Irk. Yeah, come on back," Keisha said in a fake, feminine voice, two octaves higher than her normal.

If she smiled any harder, that swig was going to pop off the top of her head.

She buzzed him back.

"Hey, Dr. Kearnan. Y'all busy?" He smiled

his sexiest smile at me. It was obvious he knew the effect he had on women.

"Hi, Eric. Things are calming down now. I just have one more patient."

"Want me to wait around until you finish?"

"That's okay. She's not going to need any lab work sent."

Keisha was standing right behind him, hoping he'd turn around and show her some more attention. She had him by at least two inches, but that didn't seem to matter to her. Keisha preferred short men. She once told me that short men have the biggest dicks. Then she pointed out his fingers stating "It's not the feet. Guuuurl, it's the hands. Look how long his fingers are."

Eric was too busy to notice Keisha stalking him. He glancing around, looking for someone else.

"Nia in today?"

"Nope, she had some things to take care of. She'll be back in tomorrow."

"Dag! Wanted to show her my new tattoo." He was visibly disappointed.

"I wanna see, Irk!"

Unaware of how close she was, he jumped. He composed himself and smiled at Keisha, but not with the same intensity as he did while mentioning Nia.

"Aight. We gonna have to go in the back 'cause it's kind of low."

That's why he was so excited about showing Niani.

Keisha could barely contain her delight. I'm sure if nobody was here, she wouldn't think twice about giving him oral sex as he lowered his pants to show his new body art. She's done worse.   Things that, unfortunately, she's never too ashamed to share with us.

They both went into one of the empty exam rooms.

"Leave it open," I yelled to them down the hall.

"Oh Dr. K., you just like somebody's mother. What do you think we gonna do?"

That fake feminine voice was grating.

"I can only imagine. Just leave it open, so Maria doesn't think there's another patient in there," I lied.

I grabbed the chart in the box on the door to the exam room. Looked over her history real quick, and went in to see my last patient for the day.

"I forgave him. We made love.
So began the cycle of my addiction."
Jaz

Chapter 4:
Jasmine

"We're still going to Tyson's Corner this weekend?"

"Yeah, Terrence is taking the girls to Six Flags. Hold on...Keisha, I need that patient's pap result ASAP. Maria, I don't have any specs in room 1. Make sure you sterilize some more before you leave. I need some more speculums for tomorrow."

Uh-oh. It sounded like Taz was really busy today.

"Nia's still going, right? I haven't heard from her since last week. I called her today, but that heifer hasn't called me back."

Taz didn't seem too interested in what I had to say.

"Negative for epithelial lesions... endocervical zone ...Huh? Oh. Yeah, she's coming. I talked to her this weekend. Some drama going on."

"What, with Cameron? Did he kirk out...?"

"No, she's fine, but...I don't have enough time to give you all the details. Yeah, I know, Yvette...Look, let me go see this last patient. I'll call you after I leave here to fill you in."

She hung up before I could say goodbye.

I was on route 450 taking the extra, extra long way home from my dad's house. I just wanted time to think clearly, before I got there. Curtis would be up by now.

Stopped at the light, I started thinking about him again, even though I was trying hard not to. I thought about the beginning of our relationship. How it started out so promising.

When you first meet someone, they have a clean slate. No marks or blemishes on their record. There's so much potential to where things could lead. I just wish I recognized the signs way back then. I should have let him go long time ago.

"Where's the Student Union?"

It was the second semester of my sophomore year at the University of Maryland in College Park when I first met Curtis. After months of getting lost and being late, I had learned to maneuver around the huge campus pretty well.

"It's right up the hill. Just past that building on the right?"

Curt was a junior, four years my senior. Transferred from Prince George's Community College. This was his first semester and he stopped me to ask for directions.

"Daaamn! I just came from my second class all the way on the other side. I'm going to be about three sizes smaller by the time I graduate here. I wish I knew all this before I transferred. I would have brought my skates."

"You're going to have to learn to plan your classes better. Make sure they're closer together, if you can help it, and give yourself time to get there if you can't."

"Okay! I'll be sure to break out my compass, protractor, and atlas next time I sign up for classes."

His playful sarcasm made me laugh. I loved a man with a sense of humor. Not to mention that he had a flawless golden-brown complexion, pretty white teeth, and dimples. His hair was in a low-cut Caesar. Brown with deep waves. He had a couple of brown freckles on his nose. 5'11". About 170lbs. Slim, but cut.

Of course, I couldn't tell that from our first meeting, but I discovered later. I also couldn't see those sexy bowlegs he was hiding in his baggy jeans. What I did see was a warm smile, kind eyes with a hint of mischief, and a playful sense of humor. I told him I had to walk that way to go to Colefield House, so I could show him. He smiled that hypnotizing, boyish smile, grabbed my bookbag for me, without asking, and followed me up that steep hill. He didn't have me at "Hello," but I was pretty much his from then on.

We ate lunch together later that day and exchanged numbers. We talked for over an hour in the dining area, and I went back to my room feeling high. Floating. Not even the snobby attitude of my stuck-up, bitchy roommate could bring me down. I spent the remainder of that night thinking about that smile.

The same night, he called me just as I had dozed off and woke me up. My heart was racing, and I was still groggy when I answered the phone. Recognition of his voice made me instantly perk up.

"I'm sorry, did I wake you?"

"No. No, not really."

"I know I said I'll call you tomorrow, but I

couldn't stop thinking about you."

"Really?" My stomach tightened in knots. I was excited to hear from him, but I didn't want him to know it.

"I don't know...I just really felt a connection today."

Me too, I thought, but I just kept silent. Trying to avoid saying anything stupid.

"Maybe we can meet tomorrow for lunch?"

"Ummm... That's cool. Same time?"

"Yeah, same time." Then he was silent for a few seconds.

"Jasmine?"

"Huh?"

"What time do you have to be up?"

"Eight, tomorrow."

"I'll call you at eight to make sure you wake up. Can't have my future teacher oversleep and miss her classes."

"Was he for real?" I thought.

"Okay. I'd really appreciate that." Earlier, at lunch, I told him I was a teaching major. He talked about the future of kids today and how important teaching was. I think he was a Social Work major at the time. Eventually, he changed to family studies and then to kinesiology before finally dropped out.

I couldn't believe he was interested in me. I thought I felt something special when we were talking during lunch. Apparently, he felt the same.

"Jasmine?"

"You can call me Jaz if you want. All my friends do."

"Okay. Jaz?"

"Yes?" I made my voice a little softer. More feminine. In a silly attempt at trying sound sexy.

"Goodnight."

"Goodnight, Curtis."

"Curt. Everybody calls me Curt."

"Okay, well, goodnight, Curt."

We hung up, and I didn't sleep a wink that night. I spent all that time thinking about him. About our conversation. How it flowed so easily. How we liked the same things. Believed in the same God. Held the same goals for marriage, family. He seemed too good to be true.

He was.

That semester was the last time I think I've been really happy.

During his free period, he would come to class with me. Most classrooms at UMD were so big, the teachers had no clue who belonged there and who didn't. We would sit in the back and write notes to each other on my notepad. He would distract me by talking about people. Sometimes he would raise his hands and ask questions like he belonged there, while I would try my best not to laugh. I ended up having to buy the notes to the class in order to pass the exams.

We would walk all over campus together talking about our dreams. We would sit next to the water fountain and hold hands. He even talked about wanting to marry me after I graduated.

The emotional chemistry was nothing compared to our physical chemistry. Mind-blowing sex was the one thing I could always count from Curt. From the first time we made love, three weeks after we first met, I was hooked.

My roommate had moved out five days prior. One of her soror's hooked her up with a room in one of the upper-class dorms on South Campus. She thought she was the shit anyway and this helped to fuel her fantasy. I would have been jealous, except it resulted in me having a room all to myself. Her arrogant attitude was never missed.

I spent those next few nights alone fantasizing about what I would do to Curtis, if we ever made it to that level. It had been so long, and I was aching for some physical intimacy. My limited sexual experience consisted of my first love, Kendrick, and a forgettable one-night stand freshman year. The latter, I don't count. Not because of Nia's well-versed motto "If I don't cum, he don't count." It's because he came before he could put it all the way in. He had managed to get the head in (after a lot of fumbling) when he let out a moan and went soft. I laid there in disbelief while he tried to explain how that never happened to him before.

Such a waste. He was one of the finest football players on the team. Built. Had a decent enough package. Nice and thick. A shame, really. I was so disgusted and embarrassed for him, I never spoke to him again. I'm not sure if his persistent phone calls were because he really liked me or because he just wanted to salvage his reputation. Either way, I refused to answer.

Valentine's day, the day we first made love, was on a Thursday. We spent most of the day together as usual and then he went to work. He hadn't given me anything, but I felt it was too soon to expect anything. Nothing was set in stone. We weren't even officially dating. Around 11pm, I answer the phone, already expecting his usual late night call. What I didn't expect was for him to tell me that he was downstairs in the lobby.

I called my girl, Anna, and asked her to let him in while I frantically changed my clothes, brushed my teeth, and removed my headscarf to comb out my wrap. I put on a cuter nightgown and some lip-gloss, to give the illusion that I always woke up looking that good. When I opened the door, he interrupted my fake yawn with a kiss. I stood there with my mouth open for a second before I noticed he had some flowers, a card, and a bottle of Alizé. I wasn't sure about it when he first called, but at that moment, I knew that I was going to give him.

Curtis came in the room and looked around. I pulled the chair out from under the desk for him, but he sat on my bed anyway. I suddenly felt very self-conscious. I worried about how I looked. If my nightie was too short. I didn't want him to get the wrong impression of me. Should I have pinned my hair up? Were my eyes too puffy? Was that sheet-wrinkle still on my cheek? What was he thinking?

I sat on the bed, facing him, glancing away nervously every so often.

"Don't be nervous. I'm sorry I came by so late. It's just...I couldn't get you out of my mind. I didn't feel right not ending Valentine's day with you."

I suddenly felt light-headed. I couldn't believe he was here telling me this.

"I know the gifts are last minute, but I didn't want to seem like I was pushing too fast. I didn't want you to think..."

I cut him off before he could finish. I leaned in, grabbed his shirt, and pulled him closer to me. I kissed him hard. Passionately. Frantically. It had been awhile since I had sex — not just sexual contact. I was anxious. Nervous. Impatient. I couldn't wait any longer.

He pushed me away slightly and cupped my face with his hands. He took control of the kiss and slowed me down. His tongue probed my mouth in a soft, gentle motion. His hands moved from my face to my hips. He pulled them towards him and guided me to standing. I stood less than an inch in front of him. The heat from his breath scorched my stomach. He placed his hands on the back of my knees and slowly glided them upwards under my nightshirt to my waist. His hands were warm. Somewhat calloused from working in a warehouse, but the roughness from his fingers was an added sensation. I felt like the nerves on my skin were hypersensitive. Every touch from him was intense. Every sensation magnified.

He lifted the fabric and exposed my stomach. Prickly gooseflesh erupted as his breath pushed against my navel and lifted the tiny hairs on my belly. My knees weakened and almost buckled when he thrust his tongue into my navel and began to lick in and out. The pleasurable sensation ran down the thin, pigmented line on my belly and ended right at the tip of my clit. It began to ache and throb, begging for attention. As if aware of the extra activity going on below, Curt reached down and massaged the sensitive flesh.

I almost lost all strength in my legs. I concentrated with every effort not to fall.

He moved my underwear to the side and opened the folds. He pulled the tiny hood of skin back until my hardened clitoris peeked out.

Gently, he rubbed the pink flesh with his thumb.

He looked up to see the expression on my face. There was no way to be self-conscious anymore. Pleasure was taking over my consciousness.

He licked my clit with his hot tongue and my knees finally gave. I had to lean forward on him for support. He grabbed my thighs and held me up. He then sat me onto the bed, laid me on my back, kneeled on the floor, and continued to consume me as if I was his last meal.

I came within seconds, but that didn't stop him. I tried to pull away, but he held on tight. I couldn't catch my breath. My heart was racing. I was coming so hard, so many times. Tears of torture and pleasure came with each orgasm. My head was pounding, but still, he wouldn't stop. Three more orgasms later, he released me from the control of his mouth.

My juices were literally dripping from his goatee. It was so much, I was embarrassed, but he never seemed to notice. He didn't bother to wipe any away, just came up to kiss me.

I hesitated for a split second, aware of my post-coital secretions on his face, but quickly got over it. I figured if it didn't bother him, it shouldn't bother me.

We kissed for what seemed like an eternity. The wait was driving me insane. The hardness from his erection was drilling a hole in my stomach. It felt large. Thick. Just the way I like them. I had to feel him inside of me.

My impatience growing, I flipped him over and climbed on top. My own aggression surprised me. I tried to calm myself before I did something I regretted.

"Do you have any condoms. There are

some Lifestyles in the other desk."

He raised his eyebrow at my comment.

"Um, from my former roommate," I added shyly.

"Don't worry.   Brought some with me just in case."

Now, I was the one to look with suspicion. He knew what I was thinking and laughed.

"I wasn't expecting anything. Just hopeful. I wanted you from the moment I saw you struggling with your books. I wanted to make sure I was prepared, in case you decided to allow me the privilege of being with you."

He reached in his back pocket and grabbed his wallet. He opened it and pulled out a Trojan's Magnum. Extra large.

Silently, I thanked the Lord.

"Can I?"

I got up. Turned the lights off. My butterfly night lamp came on automatically. The room was lit with the soft, interchanging orange, red, and blue lights.

With shaking hands, I unbuttoned and unzipped his jeans. The more I tried to control the shaking, the more obvious it seemed. I wanted to look like I was in control and confident, despite how nervous I was. I wanted to blow his mind as much as he was blowing mine.

I pulled his pants and boxers down and was greeted by a work of art. Everything about his dick amazed me. From the two-toned color of the shaft, to the winding network of bulging veins, to the swollen thickness of the head.

His manhood hung heavy between his legs, curving slightly to the left. It moved subtly, in rhythmic timing with his pulse. So deliciously perfect, I had an almost irresistible urge to take it into my mouth. Lightly grip the base while sucking on the head. Run my tongue up and down and up the length of it until he gloriously exploded in my mouth.

Wisely, I fought temptation. The reputations of other female classmates taught me never to get too freaky on the first night. Men tell you that they don't care, but they get the wrong impression if you give too much of yourself too soon.

I opened the condom and unrolled it slowly onto his penis—feeling its girth. It was all I could do to keep from throwing him on the bed and straddling him. As if reading my mind, he pulled the covers back and laid prone on my twin mattress. Needing no invitation, I climbed on top of him. Grabbing the base of his member, he held it up as I gently eased myself onto it inch by inch. A sensual moan escaped his lips as I wiggled my way down further.

He felt too good. My senses went into overload. I immediately started into a fast, offbeat ride—unable to control my pace. He grabbed my hips and forced me to slow down. His hips rose up in sync with the fall of mine to match rhythms. He controlled his entry by limiting my descent. Held my hips to keep me from moving. Then, he started deep-stroking me in a circular motion.

I was losing it. My body started to shake. Perspiration ran down my forehead. A drop hung at the tip of my nose. I was on the brink of climax when he lifted me off him.

"Wha... What are you doing?"

I wanted to cry from the abrupt break in contact. It had been too long.

"It's okay, baby. Trust me."

Not fully comprehending, I did as he said.

I sat up on the bed, so that he could move from under me. Using the reprieve to finish undressing himself, he unlaced and removed his Tims'. Slipped off his sweatshirt and then his white tee.

That was the first time I was able to view his naked slim, but cut form. Broad shoulders. Narrow hips. A small patch of hair covering the center of his chest. My eyes glanced over his chest one more time before they wandered below the waist. He stared at me for a few seconds while I stared at his dick.

I couldn't take my eyes away. Had me mesmerized. Couldn't believe that almost useless, menacing member had my eyes rolling with pleasure only a few seconds before.

Following my line of vision, he looked down, then back at me and smiled. He grabbed it. Stroked it with his hand. Circled the head with his thumb as he rounded the end. The wetness from me lubricating his stroke. Making a wet, slurpy sound.

It felt wrong. Like I shouldn't be here, watching him in my room, touching himself like that. But I couldn't turn away. It was so sexy. So erotic. So nasty. He was turning me on so much that I almost wanted to see him cum like that.

Almost.

"Come back to bed."

"Why? Don't you like watching me?"

He had a sly smile when he said this. He wanted me to beg.

"I do, but I want to feel some of that, too?"

"Feel what. What do you want to feel?"

"I want to feel you," I said timidly.

He wanted me to talk dirty, but I was uncomfortable. I wasn't used to being this forward.

This kinky.

"What do you want to feel me do, Jasmine?" He stroked a little faster.

Oh, God, he was killing me.

"I want to feel you put it in me."

"Put what in you, baby? My finger?" He pointed his index finger and held it next to his penis for comparison. Then, he chuckled.

"No!" I sucked my teeth. I was getting frustrated. Trying to form the words were difficult. "Your...your dick. I want you to put your dick inside me."

Using that word aloud embarrassed me. My face got warm. My ears started to tingle. I lowered my eyes.

"That's it. That's my girl. So tell me, how do you want it? Soft or hard? I want to know what you like. Be honest. I want you to be able to be yourself with me, baby."

His voice was low. Deep. Intoxicating.

"Soft, first...then hard." I wouldn't look at him.

"Do you like it rough?"

"No. A little...Not too much. Oh, God! Please!"

I looked up at him, impatience burning in my eyes.

"Please what? Do you want me to fuck you?"

I lowered my eyes again and nodded my head.

"Then tell me."

I shook my head, like a child denying a lie.

"Tell me."

"I...want you to f—... to fuck me."

"Don't be ashamed baby. Look at me."

I raised my eyes.

"Now, tell me again."

"I want you to fuck me. Please."

That was what he wanted to hear. He stopped pleasing himself and came over to the bed. He leaned me back and passionately kissed me. He kissed me, but he wouldn't enter me. He stimulated my lips. My tongue. Penetrated my mouth. Forced his desire into me through panting breaths.

My body was on fire. I had never met anyone like him. Instinctively, he knew my body. He was pushing me outside of my comfort zone, and I liked it. I felt like a different woman with him.

Finally, he stopped and turned me over on my stomach. He laid his body on me and kissed the small of my back. He licked all the way up to the base of my neck. Lifted my hair and kissed around my hairline. Tingles coursed throughout my body.

I was never one to explore too many sexual positions, even with my ex. But for some reason, I felt comfortable with him. Everything we did felt normal. It felt natural.

My legs parted to accommodate him, and he entered me from behind. He supported his upper body with his hands and slowly slid in and out of me. Alternating between deep penetrations to inserting only the tip, he quickly drove me to the edge.

My hands grabbed the sheets and pulled. I bit the pillow and tried to keep my moans from escaping outside of the thin walls. He started to pump harder and faster, hitting a spot that had been neglected for so long.

I came. It was short and intense – like an explosion. A hot flash accompanied it to smother the flames. Underneath me was soaked with sweat. The aftershocks left me unable to move. He kissed my neck until it was finished.

After I was done, he doubled his efforts. Again, I buried my face in the pillow. The combination of pleasure and pain making me sing again. He ran his fingers through my hair. He turned my head to the side and gave me his tongue. He was fucking me so hard, that I knew I would come again. His sweat dripped from his face into my hair.

"I love you so much, Jasmine."

Then he came, bringing me along to a heavenly climax with him.

I was too far gone at that moment to pay any attention to what he'd just told me, but I would replay those six words over and over in my head during the night after left.

He pulled out carefully so that the condom wouldn't slip off and lay beside me. I lay on my stomach, too spent to move. He grabbed my arm and pulled until I shifted my head on his chest. I was out in seconds.

I awoke to find him getting dressed.

"What time is it?"

"Shhh. Go back to sleep, Boo."

"Where are you going?   I thought you would stay the night with me?"

"You know I'm not supposed to be here this late anyway. I don't want you to get in trouble if anyone saw me leave in the morning."

"It's okay. My DA's cool."

"I still have to take my mom to work in the morning. You know we share one car since hers broke down."

"Oh, I didn't know that," I said. Disappointment was written on my face.

"Why don't you stay and just get up early

enough to take your mother to work?"

"She has to be at work by five am. If I fall asleep now, I'll probably be out until the sun comes up."

"No you won't I'll make sure you…"

"What if you don't? After what we've been doing, you'll probably be out longer than me. Besides, I'm not good sleeping in strange places."

He sounded a slightly irritated.

"Oh, so now I'm a stranger? I wasn't a stranger when you were fucking me, now was I?"

"Come on, baby, you know I didn't mean it like that. It's just that I'm only used to my own bed. Never been anywhere else for twenty-two years. When I'm at home, I sleep like a baby and wake up the same time like clockwork. When I'm somewhere else, it takes me forever to fall asleep, and then when I do, I'm so tired that I'm dead to the world. You really don't want me to risk my mom losing her job do you?"

"No."

I felt like an ass for only thinking about myself.

"Okay then. And you don't have to use that language either. You're too pretty to act like that. I can't have my girl talking like that – unless we're in the middle of making love."

He called me his girl. I couldn't believe it. All of my disappointment and shame was replaced by giddy happiness. I tried not to smile.

"Okay, baby. You're going to meet me for lunch tomorrow?"

"Of course."

He sat on the bed next to me and touched my hair, which was, by now, a curly, bushy mess.

"I love your hair. It's so pretty. So soft. You're so beautiful."

I felt myself blush. I couldn't believe him.
Even in my worst state, he thought I was beautiful.

He kissed me and whispered he loved me.
I didn't think twice before I had relied, "I love you,
too."

He left me that night on cloud nine. I
spent most of the night thinking about him again
– too excited to sleep. I had never wanted to be
with someone as much as I wanted to be with
him that night.

That truth still stands today.

This was a good time in my life. Before the
questions, and the doubts. Before the broken
promises. Before the periods of aching loneliness,
and heavy sadness. Before the inconsistent explanations and, finally, no explanations at all.

That spring semester was the beginning of
the end. We saw each other almost every day
that semester. The exceptions were weekends.
He told me that he worked a part-time job on the
weekends along with working another job some
evenings during the week. He always called me
during the week, but sometimes, it was only late
at night. I rarely heard from him on the weekends, but he claimed to be so tired, all he did was
collapse as soon as he got home. I also didn't see
him during spring break. He said that he went to
California to visit relatives.

The lack of time spent with him on the
weekends never bothered me much, since we
spent so much time together at school. We met
for lunch daily. We spent enough evenings together during the week; I never thought anything
was wrong.

I saw him even less during the summer
semester. I took an elective class to free up my

fall. He took a core class to catch up. We rarely saw each other outside of school. He worked so much, he never had any free time.

Or so he said.

We spent time together on campus and he still talked about marriage and kids. In my mind, I had our whole life together planned. I even planned my next semester around his. Scheduled our classes as the same time so that we would both be free at the same time. Even tried to make sure the classes were in buildings close together so that we could walk together.

The fall semester was where it all started to fall apart. We still walked to classes together and ate lunch, but he never stayed long on campus once his classes were done. When we went to my room, it was a quick, though always intense, lovemaking session, and then he was off. He was always doing something for somebody: Taking his mom to the store; driving one of his friends to the mall; visiting his sister in Virginia; working an extra shift for someone. It was always something.

One day, my birthday, we were supposed to go to the old BET soundstage. He said that he wanted to take me to dinner and then to the comedy show at the DC Improv. I had gone to the hairdresser and had light brown streaks put in my hair. Nia took me to the mall and she had bought me these fierce high-heel black leather boots as a present. I bought a pair of Parasuco stretch jeans that made my butt look round and a tight black sweater. I sat in my dorm—room, hair, makeup, and clothes together-and waited.

And waited.

And waited.

By 7:55pm and no phone call, I was annoyed. The show started at ten and we weren't going to have much time to eat. By 8:45, after I had already left a message, I was livid. By 10:00pm, four more messages later, I was really worried. I kept imagining that all kinds of things had happened to him. There was no way for me to find out. I didn't have his home number. I'd never been to his house. I just hoped that if something did happen to him, someone would eventually look through his phone, see all of the missed calls, and call me back to let me know the deal.

I didn't hear from him for the next two days. At first, I was relieved, then angry, when he finally called; until he told me he was calling from the hospital.

"Are you okay?! What happened? What's …"

"I'm fine. It's my mom. She's sick."

"Kidney problems" was all he would tell me. He said the doctors were really concerned. They weren't sure she would make it this time.

"That's so awful! Baby, I'm so sorry. I never knew your mom was sick. How are you doing? Where are you? Do you need anything? I can come sit with you."

"No, it's okay. My sister's here and there's a lot of family already. We're all helping each other out. I don't want you to be in this depressing environment anyway. I know how much you hate hospitals."

The first time in the hospital was seeing my grandmother dying. The last time I went inside a hospital was the last time I saw her alive. My grandmother died from breast cancer. It was eating straight through her breast by the time she finally went to the doctor. Had already spread to her brain and lungs. It killed her slowly.

Painfully.

Too young to be on the floor of the medical unit, my aunt, a nurse at the hospital, was able to sneak me in to see her after visiting hours. The last time I saw my grandmother, I barely recognized her. She was thin. Her left arm swollen to four times its size. Doped up on many painkillers, but still in pain. I could see the suffering in her eyes. I can clearly remember her eyes. And the smell. The smell of the cancer eating away her flesh mingled with antibiotics and antiseptics.

The last time they brought me in her room, I somehow knew I would never see her again. They walked me close to her bedside, and I burst into tears. She didn't remember who I was, but she still reached out to me to comfort me. She wiped my tears away and laid my head on her chest, next to the wound where her left breast had been.

I was six.

I still remember that smell.

I got a chill thinking about the hospital. The hairs on the back of my neck stood up, but I wasn't going to let that stop me from being with Curtis, if he needed me.

"I don't care about that. I care about you. I just want to make sure you're all right."

I heard a baby crying in the background. I thought about all of the children visiting sick relatives with their parents. I thought about how scared they were. And confused. How they saw their parents suffering with grief and worry, but didn't know how to make it all go away – the way that parents could make everything better when their kids were hurting.

"It's okay, baby. I don't want to have to leave my sister by herself. She needs me to be strong right now. I can worry about myself later. Plus, there're too many visitors here for my mom anyway. I'll call you later when some of the people leave and maybe you can come up."

"Okay, just call me later and let me know what's going on. Do you know how it felt to not hear a word from you in two days? I didn't know what happened to you. I was really worried."

"Oh yeah, I know. I'm so sorry about that. It's just that things got so crazy around here, I just didn't think to call. Whenever I'm worried or scared, I get kind of withdrawn. I'm truly sorry. I'll try to be more considerate next time." There wasn't a hint of sarcasm in his voice. He generally sounded sorry.

I felt like a heel again. "It's not that. I was was worried. That's all." I couldn't be mad at him with what was going on in his life. "Just call me later when you get a chance."

"I will. Oh, and Happy Birthday. I'm sorry we didn't get to go out like I planned. I promise I'll make it up to you."

"Okay, I love you."

"Love you, too."

That incident was the first of many false promises; as well as, the first of many life-threatening emergencies with his family, or himself.

Once I told the girls what had happened with Curt, they were even more wary of him.

"What kind of kidney problems?"

"I don't know. He just said kidney problems."

"Well, was it kidney failure, or kidney stones, or an infection?" Taz was a pre-med major and already trying to diagnosis something.

"I don't know, I told you. He didn't say.

Stop asking me about it." I was getting irritable. It had been four days since he called from the hospital and no word. I left a message twice telling him to call and let me know how things were going.

"I'm just trying to figure out if it's something potentially fatal or what."

"Whatever it is, I just pray that his mom is doing better."

"Whatever it is, he still could have found the time to call and let you know how he was doing. When Terrence's father died, he called Taz from the hospital, crying, not five minutes later."

Nia was suspicious from the beginning. She never trusted him. Her trusting nature didn't prevail when dealing with Curtis. What she couldn't see when it came to her own affairs, was clear as crystal when it came to mine. She was the first to voice suspicion about how he was making future wedding plans with me and had yet to introduce me to his mother.

I didn't want to hear any of her negative comments right now. It just added to my own nagging doubts. "I don't want to talk about him right now. Are we going to the step show after the game? You know there's going to be some cute guys there."

Taz had looked at me like she wanted to say something, but didn't. She had that look of pity on her face that I'd seen on many of occasions. I didn't need that from her. I was getting irritated with all of them.

"For real, though! You know my fine-ass Sigma's are going to bring the house down." My friend, Carmen, came out of nowhere and bust into our conversation.

"Ewww. That bunch of pretty-boy wannabe's? I'll be looking for my Q-dogs to come in and regulate," Nia said with disdain.

Nia and Carmen always disagreed about which group of guys were cuter. Sigma's or Q's. Football team or the basketball team. Maryland or DC. Liberal arts majors or science and arts majors. It didn't matter.

I interrupted their banter before it turned into another full-fledged debate. "A-ny-way, I got the tickets to the game. Are we gonna meet at the Union?"

"I'll be there after I get back. Mannie is taking me to the mall." Nia smiled as she said this.

It was hard keeping track of Nia's male friends. She called them all her brothers, but I know most, if not all, were contemplating incest on a daily basis.

Taz rolled her eyes and questioned Niani. "Which one is Mannie?"

She sucked her teeth. "Tsk. Stop playin'. You know the one with the brother that owns that car detailing shop."

"Oh, yeah! Him." I still had no clue who he was, but didn't feel like getting into it. "Oh, guess who I ran into the other day? James Wright. From Lanham."

Nia wrinkled her nose at the mention of his name. "James that went to high school with us? Wasn't he like a senior in high school when we were freshman?"

"Yeah, and didn't he hustle big time?" Taz piously added.

"Well, he's not hustling now," I added. He started his own clothing line. I think Rugged House Wear or something."

"I seen a couple of guys wearing those

shirts before. Mainly in DC," Carmen added.

"Anyway, he asked about you, Nia."

"Me? What did he say?"

"Yeah, what did he say?" Carmen echoed, gaining an eye-roll from Niani.

Carmen could be such a bugaboo sometimes, and today was no different. My patience was paper-thin. Her buoyant energy, which normally kept me entertained, was grating my nerves.

"He wanted to know how you were doing. He asked for your number."

"You didn't give it to him did you?"

"Yeah. Why? I thought you thought he was cute back in the day."

"I did, but he was annoying. Always thought he was the shit. I didn't really know him too well personally, but he had that arrogant attitude that I can't stand. Most pretty-boys do."

"What have you got against pretty-boys?" Carmen interjected.

"I just can't have no nigga walking around thinking he looks better than moi."

I couldn't stand the thought of those two starting up, so again, I interrupted. "A-ny-way, he didn't seem arrogant. He actually said he had gotten saved two years ago, and he straightened his life up." Nia gave me the "Who cares?" roll of the eyes.

I sighed. "To sum it all up, he'll be calling soon."

I had become impatient with the entire conversation, so I abruptly walked away. Nia looked a little pissed, but I couldn't worry about that now.

He really did seem like a nice guy, plus he and Curtis knew each other from Prince George's

Community College, so I gave him her number without her permission. Maybe I shouldn't have, but it was too late to do anything at that time.

My mind kept focusing on Curtis and why hadn't he called. It wasn't until the following evening that I heard from him. He said his mother was out of the hospital and recovering fine. He apologized profusely for not contacting me that whole time. He talked about how much he missed me and needed to see me. I was too happy to be angry and invited him over without hesitation.

I forgave him.

We made love.

So began the cycle of my addiction.

"All I could think about was his hands, his mouth, his
lips.
Cameron."
Nia

Chapter 5
Niani

"I'm about to go to the barber shop. If you
want, I'll take your car and get it washed."

James walked directly in my line of vision.
Blocking my view of The Chappell Show. The
kids puppet show episode.

"That's okay." I looked to the left of him to
see the screen. I was trying to concentrate on the
show. Not purposely trying to annoy him, I just
wanted to avoid him.

"Nia."

"Hmmm?" My face turned up to meet his,
but my eyes absently remained on the screen. I
could hear the jokes, but my mind didn't register
any of them. I laughed on cue with the audience.

"Look at me, please."

He gently touched my face to get my attention. The touch was like a snap breaking me out
of my trance. My protective shield wavered a little, and I looked up to face him. His hazel eyes
pleaded with me for acknowledgement. Understanding. Reassurance.

In my best, loving voice, I responded. "I'm
sorry, baby. What is it?"

Lines formed across his head as he furrowed his brows. He could see something in my eyes that I was trying to hide. Heard something in my voice that I was trying to conceal.

I started to panic. Did he know something? I didn't want him to see what I tried so hard to hide.

"Are you okay, Nia? You've been acting a little strange since that accident. I know you were upset, but it's not like somebody d—um...What's wrong with you? Talk to me. You barely say three words to me at a time, and that's really unlike you not to talk. You barely look at me. You stare at that damn TV more than you do me. And the car...it still has blood on it. It's almost been a week."

The concern in his voice stung. He'd been trying his best to not upset me and give me my space. I've been so focused on my own emotional turmoil that I never noticed what he was going through – seeing me like this.

I tried my best to reassure him.

"You know how much I love animals, Jay. It's just that I never killed another living creature before – except bugs. Even then, I say I'm sorry."

"I know. I know. I just don't like seeing you like this. You're scaring me. Even worse than you did that night."

That night, I came in the apartment hysterical. James was in a rage that I didn't return his calls. I was crying, rambling, stuttering all kinds of nonsense. Survival instinct took over where my mind had left, and I somehow managed to spit out a lie about me working late in the office to help Taz. I told him the cell phone was in the car. The post-crying hiccups had left me barely able to speak. When I mentioned having an accident, he freaked.   His anger instantly turned to fear and concern.   Over and over, he asked me if I was okay.   Made me sit down. Forced me to stumble out the details.

I had never seen him so attentive. So affectionate. After I cried and gave him the details, he started hugging me. Kissing me. Thanking God that I was okay. I returned his kisses, desperately trying to feel something other than emotional pain. My eagerness surprised him, but he accepted it without hesitation. He carefully undressed me making sure I wasn't hurt anywhere. He bathed me, dried me off, and carried me to bed like a child.

We slowly, carefully made love. I let him take the lead. The tender kisses and gentle caresses numbed the pain in my heart for awhile, but the guilt remained. I worked feverously towards an orgasm to gain some much-needed relief. I cried so hard when I came that he stopped, laid beside me, and held me until I cried myself to sleep.

James never asked me what upset me so bad. I never asked him why he came back so early. That thought never crossed my mind. It was preoccupied.

All I could think about was his hands, his mouth, his lips.

Cameron.

It was over two weeks since I last talked to him. He called every morning and every evening for the first five days straight, but I refused to answer. I would look at the phone, fighting the urge to press talk, until the missed call symbol popped up. Then, I would check the message and fight again not to call him back. What started out as long, caring messages got shorter and colder each time. His feelings for me hardening like plaster:

> *"Nia, I know you're upset and probably a little confused right now, but call me back. I want to talk to you. We...We need to talk about this. I love you so much and I can't...I don't want to let you go like this. Please call me in the morning."*

> *"Nia, call me back. I want to make sure you're all right. I'm worried about you, baby. I miss you. Please give me a call when you can. Let me know what's up. Peace."*

> *"Babygirl, you know who this is. Thinking about you. Don't shut me out. We need to talk."*

> *"I'm just calling to check up on you. See how you're doing. Hit me back."*

> *"This is Cameron. I'm not trying to bug you. I'm just...Call me back."*

> *"Hey...um...at least let me know you're still alive."*

After listening to each message two, maybe three times, I deleted them. I didn't want to risk saving them and replaying them over and over. Feeding into my desire to hear him in real-time—maybe even in person.

His last message was yesterday. Only two words, they were all that was needed to convey his message.

> *"You win."*

It was still the same calm, deep voice that

had swayed me for the past year. But, the resignation in it surprised me. Always confident, I had never heard him sound defeated. It hurt more than I thought it would.

I listened to that message once, because I couldn't bear to hear it again. With a lump in my throat and tears in my eyes, I pressed save.

James broke me out of my reflective trance again.

"Baby!"

"I'm sorry. I just keep thinking about it, I guess. It's nothing serious." I forced myself to smile and infused my face with false emotion. "Don't be so worried." Tried to look more human than robot.

James stared back as if he didn't believe me.

"Really, I'm okay. But, If you don't mind, I would appreciate you getting my car washed. I hadn't noticed the blood."

That was a lie. I saw the blood every time I went to the car. Sometimes, I stared hard out the window to find the stains on it. The dried blood helped me to remember. Maybe that accident was a wake-up call. Maybe that dog was a symbol that that could be me. If I continued the way I was living. Lying dead in the road.

Except, I felt dead already. These three weeks not talking to Cameron had been worse than death.

I felt empty.

The arrival of my long awaited period wasn't enough to pull me out of this sadness. In fact, I was a little disappointed.

"What's wrong with me?"

Something's missing. Something that I

need to function properly is gone. When did this happen? When did he become such a vital part of my being?

Why did I let this get so deep?

"All right, Nipsy. I'll be back in a few."

He called me "Nipsy." The worry in his mind was easing. Nipsy, his pet name for me, came from when we first started dating. He used to tease me about my nipples saying that they were almost as big as my breasts. It's a name he uses when he's in a good mood.

"Sure you don't want to come?"

Actually, I was very sure. The longer I was around him, the longer I would have to keep up this front. I had to use some reverse psychology.

"Ummm...okay. But you'll have to wait for me to get ready, first. I haven't showered yet, and I want to do my hair. I should only be about..."

"Whoa! That's okay. I don't have four hours to wait for you." He laughed and kissed me.

I kept playing the part. "It does *not* take me that long. Stop playin'!"

"Whatever, girl! It takes you an hour alone just to shower. Shit, you need to get all cute just to go outside and get the mail. I don't even know why it takes you so long anyway. As short as you are, it should take you half the time it takes a normal woman to get dressed."

Not as tall as Cameron, at barely six feet even, James still had me by a foot.

"What are you trying to say?" I threw a pillow at his head and missed.

"All I'm saying is why does it take four hours for a midget to put on her clothes? Wait. Maybe it's because of those stubby little hands and fingers of yours." I swung at him and missed again. He reached over the couch, held my wrists with one hand, and started tickling me.

Laughing, eyes filling with tears from the sensation, I admitted defeat. "All right! Stop! Stop! You win! I'll wait here! You win!" I hated being tickled.

"All right, boo. I'm gone. I'll be back." He kissed me real quick before he let go of my wrists and darted out the front door. It closed just in time to keep the pillow from connecting with the back of his head.

I waited with a half-smile on my face until I heard the engine of his gold-mist Escalade come to life and, then, fade away in the distance.

My face relaxed into a blank expression.

"You win."

I repeated Cameron's message to no one in particular. As if on cue, I started to cry silently. Tears rolled down my face undisturbed. The salt taste filling the back of my throat made me want to choke.

My feelings could no longer be contained. Like a pressure valve releasing tension, a fragile hoarse whisper escaped my mouth before I could catch it.

"Cameron."

It was involuntary.

Like my love.

I couldn't control it no matter how badly I wanted to.

"...I was tired of being pacified."
Jaz

Chapter 6
Jasmine

My condo is little, but cozy. I don't need much space. It's just me. And Curt, when he's around. For the past month, we've been more on than off.

Before, I would have thanked God every night that he was here with me. Now, the more he's around, the more depressed I become.

As soon as I stepped through the door, the disheveled state of my normally immaculate house upset me. A plate was sitting in the dining area housing two fruit flies. He had left his dirty dishes on the table again.

Not too long ago, I used to cheerfully clean up behind him like a privileged house slave. There were no drawers too dirty, no glass too sticky, no carpet too stained that I wasn't all too happy to clean. They meant that Curtis had been here. That he had been a part of my world.

Now, his carelessness is just a symbol of his feelings for me. No consideration. No thought. No effort.

I wanted to take that plate. Throw it and the half-eaten steak to the wall. Smash it into sharp pieces.   Grab the largest piece with a sharpest edge. Go in the room and slice a jugular while he's sleeping.

Maybe Lorena-Bobbit him instead.

Let him live for the rest of his life with a fraction of the pain he's caused me.

He would be getting off lucky.

My pain cuts way deeper.

A calm, relaxing sensation ran through my body as I thought about severing the source of my greatest pain and pleasure.

Provoked by one dirty plate.

"Hey, baby."

He stepped out of the bedroom yawning. Face slightly puffy from sleep. Wearing nothing but a pair of boxer briefs. His post-sleep erection tilting firmly to the left.

Despite the disgust I felt, my heart still jumped at the sight of him. I felt like Pavlov's dog, salivating at the sound of the dinner bell. My body betrayed my mind once again. He's just. So. Sexy.

I turned away from him to dull the effect. Let him face the back of my head.

"Hey," I said blankly.

"That's my wifey. Working out all early in the morning. Keeping that body tight for me."

I hate the term "wifey." A junk title created to make women feel special, with no real meaning, power, or status behind it. A pacifier. And I was tired of being pacified.

He put his arms around me and kissed me on the cheek. His morning breath singed my nostrils.

His morning erection seared my backside.

"Early in the morning? It's after twelve," I thought.

I tensed up and pulled away.

"I'm all sweaty. I really need to get in shower right about now."

"Now that you mention it, I think I need to take a shower, too."

My body wanted to weaken, but I wouldn't give in.

"Don't worry. I won't be long."

He came back behind me and caught me in another embrace. His hands slid between my legs and started massaging my clitoris.

"You will once I get in there."

I turned around to try to push away, and he slid his hands down to my butt and grabbed firmly. His erection pressed into my pubic bone. Unbelievable heat radiated from it. My resolve was wavering. I had ten seconds of self-control remaining.

"Don't do that." I moved his hands from my ass. "I want to shower by myself. I need to... meditate on things. Got a lot on my mind."

"I can help take those things off of your mind for you."

"I don't need you..." I stopped myself. "I don't need your help. These are things I need to deal with myself."

I looked directly at him trying to drive my point through.

He remained clueless. As always, too involved in himself to notice anything wrong with me.

"Come on baby. You know I don't like to shower by alone."

"Oh? Then how do you shower when you're not staying with me? How do you get by during those long stretches of time that I don't see or hear from you? When you say you need to be by yourself to "regenerate"? What do you do when you need to shower then?"

That made him uncomfortable.

It was my own fault. He wasn't used to me questioning his whereabouts like that.

He laughed nervously. "Where is all this coming from? Look, you're obviously tired and not in a very good mood. I'd be irritable too if I got up as early as you did just for some exercise. Take your shower by yourself. Take all the time you need to get in a better mood. I'll be waiting to rub your back when you finish."

"That's it. Change the subject. Ignore the obvious—that I'm tired of your bitch-ass! I'm tired of your lies! Tired of you being broke! Not keeping a job! Playing me for an idiot!"

I wanted to yell all of these things to him, but the fight had left me. I had somewhat of a victory. A very small one.

Now all I wanted was to rinse the residue of sweat and tears off my body. Detox my system starting from the outside, in.

"It was getting deeper than I was willing to go."
Taz

Chapter 7
Tazanna

"Don't worry. I don't plan on having sex until well after the six weeks."

Mrs. Wallace was 38 years old. This was her 4th child. Unplanned. She has a 13 month old and a 3-year-old from her second husband. A 16-year-old from her first.

"That's what we all say. Then we forget. Remember that little one you have at home."

"How can I forget? She is not going to be happy when I bring home her little brother."

"Not that. Remember how you said that your husband wasn't getting anywhere near you after she was born?'

"And look at me, I mean, us now."

"Well, I'm giving you condoms just in case you have a temporary lapse in your memory."

"Thank you. I'll keep them close by. Just in case."

"Just in case, huh?"

We laughed.

She was one of those patients you loved to see. Like seeing an old friend. Nothing but good memories and laughs. She was married. Employed in the government. Strong Christian woman. Husband very supportive. Children always clean and cared for. And she delivered them fast. No 24 hour labors for her. Less time in the delivery room for me.

"Remember to make an appointment in six weeks."

I left out of the room and went to the nurse's station. The floor didn't look too busy tonight. Just had to finish my charting and I was out of here.

"Hey Dr. Kearnan. I didn't know you were here. Did you see Tanya Morris yet?"

Reese, one of the LDRP nurses, greeted me with her usual pleasant demeanor. She was around my age. Short. Brown-skinned. Average build. Her hair in short natural twists. From somewhere in New York. Long Island, if I remember.

"Yeah. I already saw her. Her incision looks okay."

"Did she tell you that she wanted to switch pain medications? The Percocet makes her nauseous."

"No, she sure didn't. I'm sure she wanted to wait until I left, then ask you about it at two in the morning so that you would have to page for some Tylenol #3."

She laughed as she put her chart down in front of me. "You know how these patients are. They complain about a million things to their nurse and as soon as the doctor shows up, they don't need anything." She had already written out an order for Tylenol #3. All I had to was add my John Hancock.

"I hear you."

"Let me get her some pain medicine now.

I'll see you."

"All right, girl. See you tomorrow."

"Not me, you won't. I am off, thank Gawd." Her Long Island accent was thick today. It made her sound like an old Jewish woman.

Reese was real cool. Most of the nurses here were. I loved to sit at the nurse's station and hear some of the stories they tell. Sometimes about crazy patients. Sometimes about crazy staff. There was always some drama going on in 2-North.

Today wasn't the day to sit and socialize. I wanted to finish my work and get home to my family. I walked into the dictation room to do my charting in peace just as my phone rang. Embarrassed by the Jamie Foxx "Blame It" ring tone, I silenced before any patients could hear.

Once I recognized the number, I could barely hold back a huge grin. I looked around to make sure no one else was in the dictation room with me.

I tried to sound casual as I answered.

"Hello?"

"Hey. Where are you?"

The voice on the other end switched me into another mode.

My lover owns a raspy, smoky voice.

"At the hospital finishing my charting. I'm almost done. You?"

"I just got on route 50. Why? Do you want to hook up?"

"*Hell yeah, I want to hook up! It's been a minute,*" I thought.

"Can't. Terrence rented a movie. It's so rare when he can spend time with me. You know I have to treat it like a special event." A talented neurosurgeon, my husband worked long hours at the county hospital.

"Why don't I meet you at the hospital, then? Out back. I really want to see you."

"It can't be too long. He'll be expecting me by 9:45, 10 o'clock."

"Then I won't keep you long. Just needed to see you. Alone. It's been a rough week. Same place out back?"

"Yeah. The back parking lot. I'll be there in fifteen minutes."

"I'll be there in ten."

It was getting dark. The only things left of the preceding sunset were the reddish-orange hues lining the horizon. I drove my Highlander up the hill to the overflow parking lot behind the hospital. Day shift over and evening shift coming to an end, the lot was nearly empty. The only car left was a huge gas-guzzling SUV. Engine still running. Music loud enough to hear the bass through closed windows.

My lover drives a midnight blue, Lincoln Navigator.

I parked my car next to it. Got out and walked over to the passenger side. The temperature had lowered considerably, but the humidity made it so that one could barely tell. I was already feeling sticky.

Blessed cool, conditioned air greeted my face, arms and legs as I climbed into the waiting vehicle.

"Your locks are getting long. You just had them twisted?" I tried casual conversation to mask the nervous energy I felt creeping on me.

"Yeah, Trisha tightened me up yesterday. It was last minute, but she met me at the shop after closing time. Was talking my head off. I didn't leave the shop until well after midnight. She said she needed some company, anyway. Someone to talk to."

A tinge of jealousy made me bristle. Where did that come from?

"You look nice in your skirt, Taz."

"You look tired."

"Ha, ha! Very funny. Don't start with me."

"You need to drink some more water. Stop eating so much junk. How are things at the Center?"

"Crazy as usual. I had a crash c-section. Only three other doc's were on the floor. One was busy in a delivery. The other two were doing a c-section in the second OR. I had to do the procedure with a nurse midwife as first assist, and an inexperienced RN as scrub tech. The baby was rushed to NICU with 3/5 Apgars. Luckily she stabilized and was doing pretty good when I left. Days like this make me wonder why I let you talk me out of going into Dermatology."

My lover chose the same college and the same profession as I.

"Oh, I'm sorry. Didn't mean to point the gun at your head as you decided on your specialty. It's not like it was loaded or anything." Sarcasm was my safety net.

I looked out the window because I wasn't sure what else to say

I joked because I was nervous. We were talking, but talking was not what I wanted to do at that moment. I had little time and even less patience.

As if my mind was being read, I felt a hand on my chin, turning my face in the opposite direction. Lips pressed onto mine. A warm tongue traced the inside of them before entering my mouth.   The hand that was on my chin, moved slowly down my neck and then, inside my shirt. It squeezed my breast gently through the bra before slipping underneath, finding my nipple.   A small moan escaped me.

My lover is blessed with the softest lips I have ever tasted.

No sooner than I had made that sound, the hand stopped.   It pulled away, returning to its side of the vehicle.   Eyes looked seductively at me. Teasing me. Inviting me.

I did the only thing I could do then.   I returned the favor.

I leaned over and put my mouth on the soft skin of a long neck.   Focused my attention on the sensitive area just beneath the ear.   Licking and biting it.   My hand grabbed the other side then slid down, underneath the scrub top.   It reached in, cupped a breast as warm and as full as mine. Took the nipple and gently rolled it between two fingers.

My lover is the most tantalizing woman I have ever met.

Her soft whimpers do something to me. Change me. Turn me into a different person.

At work, the female body is just another specimen.   No special allure. Nothing to get excited about.   The same things that I have, in different sizes, shapes, and colors.

But her? Her female body is mesmerizing. Addicting.

At work, I'm around so many vaginas that the smell gets in my pores.   The first thing I want to do when I get home is shower and rub menthol under my nose.

Her smell is intoxicating.

So many times, I've buried my nose deep

into her soft mound of hair and breathed in as much as my lungs could hold. I would smell my fingers afterwards to reminisce from the faint scent left behind – reluctant to wash them.

I let my fingers lazily wander now to that magic cove. They take their time, finding detours along the way. Moving around to palm the small of her back. Rounding the front to massage a thumb into her navel. Climbing up to again feel the heaviness of her soft breasts. They pretend that they're lost. Wandering aimlessly along the landscape of her body. Pausing at rest stops on the way to their final destination.

She's taught me well.

Our first sexual encounter consisted mostly of her giving and me receiving. I was shy. Scared. Nervous. Guilt-ridden and excited all in one. She was the teacher. The seductress. I, the novice. I was completely under her control. But now...

I tugged at the bowknot of her scrub bottoms until the strings gave and the material loosened. My fingers suddenly remember their direction, slipping inside her pants. She parted her knees slightly to show me she wanted my intrusion.

I accepted her invitation and found that she was waiting for me – no underwear there to hinder access. The area of soft tight curls was damp.

Hot.

The area below it was wet. Folds slick with perspiration and excitement. I found her clitoris, careful not to scratch the sensitive skin with my manicured nail. Used the pad of my index finger, moisture from her secretions, and a soft circular motion to make my lover lose her composure.

The flesh hardened beneath my finger. I used two fingers and massaged a little firmer. Her legs opened a little wider.

My two fingers slid down and glided easily into her opening. The muscles tightened around them. I pushed them as far as they could go, then, massaged them into the spongy flesh just behind the pubic bone. My thumb reached up and tended to the neglected clitoris. The combination of stimulation always brought her to climax quickly. This was no exception. The muscles gripping my fingers turned into a vice. The spasm of an orgasm from her organ echoed throughout her whole body as her short repetitive sounds turned into one long moan.

I loved to make her cum, but was disappointed that it couldn't have been with my tongue. I longed to taste her. Smell her. This just wasn't the time or the place.

"God, you don't know how much I wanted that! I've been thinking about you so much lately. Needed to cum so bad." She reached out and turned the AC to high. "It's not even the same with Jason anymore." She adjusted herself and slid back up in her seat. "I have to pretend it's you touching me in order to cum, and lately that hasn't been working."

"Really?" Her words hit a nerve. Made me a little uncomfortable. I wish I could say the same, but the sex between Terrence and I was never an issue. Being with her makes me excited me. I get even hornier for him. I started fidgeting and looking away. When she talked like this, it made me nervous.

I wanted to change the subject slightly. It was getting deeper than I was willing to go. I preferred shallower waters when dealing with her.

"Yeah, I could tell it's been awhile, since came so hard.   But...uh...You know I have to go now. Terrence will be calling any minute now."

"Uh-Uh.   Not before I get what I really came for."

With that, she leaned all the way over and used the control to lean my seat back.

"Wait, we can't..."

"Shhhhhh...."

Her hands were already on my thighs. Face very close to my flesh. When she shushed me, the breeze from her mouth caressed my skin. The tension I felt melted away in seconds.   My eyes closed as I anticipated the feel of her soft tongue.   Its wetness and warmth.   My clit throbbed in beat with my pulse. It, also, anticipated her tongue.

Through closed eyelids, I could see light coming from my right.   Quickly, I opened them and sat up. Corrine sat upright also. We both saw the security jeep drive through the parking lot. The guard making his routine patrol of the hospital grounds barely glanced our way.   He looked at the truck and the two women sitting inside, saw no obvious signs of disturbance, and continued his rounds with disinterest. He didn't notice that my seat was still leaning back or that Corrine was leaning slightly in my direction. He didn't notice the look of guilt on our faces.

Had he come through just a minute later, he would have gotten a lot more excitement out of his normal routine. I would have been too involved to notice approaching lights. I wondered for a second if he had seen us in the act, would he have stopped us or stayed to watch until we noticed? Or would he have kept going out of embarrassment, slowing down just enough on his way out to see some of the show?

I put my seat up and adjusted my skirt.

"Um, I really have to go." Before she could respond, I opened the door and stepped out. I couldn't give her a chance to change my mind.

"I'll call you in the morning. Maybe we can go to the spot this weekend."

The look of disappointment she gave me held a tinge of something else. Hurt, maybe? I couldn't tell. Honestly, I didn't think I wanted to. I broke eye contact as quick as I could, and hurried into my car. My ignition turned and the engine purred. I turned down the hill, on the way out of the parking lot without glancing in my rearview.

"I need to step my game up."
Nia

Chapter 8:
Niani

"I'm really not in the mood for socializing tonight." Even en route to the club, I was trying to worm my way out of going. Taz was not backing down.

A few years ago, we all agreed to hook up at least once a month to bond and let off steam. Never just one specific meeting place. Sometimes we go out to a club, restaurant, or bar. Sometimes we just bring food and alcohol to somebody's house to eat, drink, vent, watch videos, and laugh until our stomach hurts. Once in awhile we'll invite a mutual friend outside the main circle, but mostly, it's just us three.

Tonight, we're going to Club Amor.

"I don't care what you feel like, you're coming. I arranged this weeks ago. Besides, you've been sulking all month. You need to get out and exhale, girl! The bonds of sisterhood heal all wounds."

Taz sounded tipsy already. Girlfriend has been reading one too many Iyanla Vanzant self-help books.

"But Taz, really, I..."

"You're coming. Get over it. We'll be near the back." She hung up before I could reply.

I gave up on finding a good excuse, and figured hanging out wouldn't be as bad as sleeping alone again tonight. James was on another business trip, and I really needed his company. It was going on two weeks since he went to Jersey to check on his business. Since I was on my period, I couldn't even get a goodbye quickie before he left.

I rubbed my thighs as I thought about wrapping my legs around his strong waist.

My phone went off again. I didn't recognize the number, but since it was a Jersey area code, I answered anyway. I was rewarded with hearing James' sexy voice on the other end.

"Hey, babe, what are you doing?"

Hearing his voice made me smile.

"Hey, sweetie! What number are you calling me from?"

"This is Donovan's house phone. I lost my cell while I was out, so call me here if you need me. I'm getting a new phone as soon as the mall opens, tomorrow."

"You make sure you do that, punk. Your ears must have been burning, because I just had a mental of that in time up in Westminster. Remember, when we made love for three hours?" I started to blush thinking about him again.

"Shoot, how could I forget? I wore you out that night, girl! Three rounds with me, and you were sleeping like a baby. You just best be ready to try for four rounds when I get back."

"Whatever, boy! You could barely hang in round three the way I was riding Big Daddy. Anyway, what are you doing now?"

"I have to head back out to Black Diamonds. The lights don't work in the bathroom, and I have to meet the electrician."

Black Diamonds is the laundromat he opened in New Jersey last month. He already co-owned a barbershop there with his brother. After his manager, who was also his cousin, mishandled a few major things, he went up there to check on him.

"Have you straightened things out with all of your business affairs?"

"Almost, but I'm going to have to go by the barber shop before I do come back home. Something's not right with my money, and I need to go over the books. I hate crunching numbers, but I gotta make sure my shit is straight."

One thing about James – he was good with numbers. He never had a problem making money.

I just wished he would stop relying in his family members to run his businesses and hire a professional. One of them was always doing him dirty.

Better yet, I wished he would stop opening businesses so far from home.

"Are you still staying with your brother or are you going to a hotel?"

"With my brother. He and his wife were on vacation this week, so I had the place to myself. They should be getting back sometime early in the morning. Why? Are you gonna come and stay with me this weekend? I can rent a room and so we can start round four early?"

"Mmmmm. Don't tempt me. You know my cousin's baby shower is on Sunday. My aunt would kill me if I didn't show up for her first grandbaby's shower. Plus she thinks she's Martha Stewart, so she wants to impress everyone with her skill."

"I know, I know. I was just hoping you would change your mind. You have fun tonight, baby, and be safe. Don't let me find out some nigga was freakin' on you or I'll bring so much drama, Love will have to change their name a second time."

"Whatever, punk, I'll freak on whoever I like."

"And you'll be adding to DC's murder rate." He didn't laugh as he said this, but I knew he was playing. James has a reputation from his old street life, but he is far from insecure. Me, dancing with other men never bothered him. In fact, I kind of think it turns him on because he lets— damn near encourages—me to dance with other men when I'm with him.

"Okay, baby, I have to park. I'll call you later."

"Okay, Nips. Love you."

"Love you too."

I really did love James. I just wished he wasn't so busy all the time with work. It left me with many lonely nights thinking about him.

New York Ave was congested with cars. A combination of rush hour stragglers, after-work socialites, and early club hoppers made traffic a bitch on Friday nights. I had to break suddenly to avoid rear-ending the Caprice in front of me who had stopped for a parking space. The driver continued to blast Go-go and yak in his cell as I drove past – pissed.

I pulled in front of the club around 9:40 and left my car with the valet. The foreign and, I assumed, Ethiopian valet greeted me with an overeager smile. His accent was thick, but he tried to make casual conversation. He made a friendly joke about the inside of my car being junky with all kinds of papers. I didn't respond.

There was a line forming already. A number of women and a handful of men moved orderly towards the entrance. Some were engaged in conversation. Some were busy checking out the prospects. Most were checking out the competition. A group of four women (all looking like they came straight from work) were inspecting the outfits of the two women in front of them. The manner in which they leaned into each other to talk, smirked, and covered their mouths made it obvious that they weren't paying compliments.

I couldn't remember if somebody famous was performing or not, but the crowd outside, and the fact that valet parking was $20 dollars this early in the evening were both signs that pointed to "yes." I didn't have to wait long to gain entry. The VIP line was short.

The usual glances and smiles in my direction started as soon as I stepped through the door. I wasn't in the mood tonight. Out of the corner of my eye, I could see men casually try to make their way towards me. In situations like this, I've learned to avoid direct eye contact at all costs. For most guys, even a split second is enough of an invitation to come over.

"Are you looking for someone?"

A small high-yellow man decided to be first one brave enough to test the waters. He grabbed my arm and halted my journey to find my friends. His touch was gentle enough, but I wasn't one to tolerate uninvited physical contact. A light red mist began to cloud my vision. I looked him up and down—my displeasure obvious, but Mini-me clueless. This brother had the nerve to be wearing what appeared to be a Coogi sweater vest over a bare chest. It was 97 degrees outside, and he came in here with a sweater vest, a bird-chest, and twig-arms? Not to mention his glasses were so thick, he could see the future.

Irritation caused the muscles of my face to tense up. I grit my teeth in a last minute effort to hold back a verbal assault. Oblivious, he smiled me, ignorant of what was about to come, and said,

"Maybe I can help you."

My mouth opened, ready to light into his ass, when fate intervened on his behalf. Jasmine rescued me and him by calling out my name. I looked over and saw my girls sitting on the lounge chairs in the corner. He followed my gaze and looked back to see them also. Disappointed and not into mackin' in front of an audience, his confidence immediately fizzled.

"Thanks, but no." I smiled my best sarcastic smile, yanked my arm away, and walked to the back.

Taz had paid for a VIP section so that we could sit, order food, and talk about people in comfort. VIP sections didn't come cheap in this camp, but Money-earnin' Taz Kearnan could afford it. I thought about the advantages of having two doctors in the house.

"Must be nice."

The familiar pang of jealousy ignited my brain, but guilt quickly stamped it out. After all she's done for me after everything I've done to her, I had no right to think anything negative about her. She was my best friend and my sister. She was also my sometimes overbearing mother.

"There I go again."

The heat, the crowd, and lack of sex had put me in a foul mood. I hated feeling any resentment towards her. It wasn't fair. Her life was far from perfect. We all have our skeletons. Our crosses to bear. I glanced at the floor in shame.

"Gurrl, hurry up and sit down before you send Frodo out of here crying. Did you see that? He had no clue who he was trying to push up on."

Jaz's smile dissolved my guilt and irritation. My mood lightened and, instantly, I was grateful that I came. She had been so down lately, it was good to see her happy for once. That worthless fraction of a man had been breaking her spirit one piece at a time. But, today, she seemed different.

"If you didn't call her when you did...Lord!" My model-beautiful mother-figure stood up on endless legs to hug me before I sat down.

"You better had shown up." She whispered in my ear before she sat back down.

My girl was doing it up tonight. Her hair, done in a loosely-waved bob, was immaculate. Her makeup—shimmery green shadow, mascara, bronzer, and clear lipgloss—was as flawless as her naked skin. She had on low-rise, skinny jeans, stiletto heels, and a loose-fitting, off-the-shoulder peasant top that still couldn't hide her generous cleavage. Contacts replaced the spectacles she kept over her hazel eyes. She actually looked her age, instead of ten years older. I was impressed. Tazanna (a Native American name for princess) was living up to her name.

"Why is it so packed tonight? The line was around the corner."

"Nate is performing tonight?"

Jasmine's eyes lit up at the sound of this.

"My boo-boo is performing? Now how come he didn't tell me?"

"Probably, because he doesn't know you,"

Taz said after taking a long sip of her drink. "And he never will – as shy as you are."

"Watch, the next time I see him at the gym I'm going..."

"You're going to stare at him with your mouth open like you do every other time you see him," I chimed in. Taz and I laughed and slapped each other fives.

"Whatever, Nia. He's just so much finer in person. But I'm going to get past all that, just wait!"

Jaz looked good with a short skirt that showed her thick, shapely legs and a beautifully designed, open-back shirt that discreetly showed a glimpse of her toned stomach. Her thick, jet-black hair was flat-ironed straight and rested in the middle of her back, just above the partially visible tribal tattoo. Skin tanned by her morning jogs in the summer sun. She was looking very Somalian, today. The smooth brown skin on her face was practically glowing while mine was blotchy and dull, with a pimple forming right on the chin.

I actually felt like the dowdy one today. My gray pencil skirt, black camisole, and black hat made me look practically Amish next to those two.

I need to step my game up. I hate to be outdone.

"What the hell did that hobbit have on? You were close to that creation. What was it?"

"Girl, I don't know. I think he couldn't bear to part with his Coogi sweater in the summer time, so he made a vest out of it. Ewww!"

"Doesn't he know, like, Coogi is sooo 2007?" Jaz said in her impeccable Valley-girl accent.

We all laughed.

Taz joined in with her with her best Sha-Nay-Nay/hoodrat impression. "Umm hmmm, for real, doe. Who be werrin' "Coochie" now anyways? He needs to go buy him summa dat Sean Paul or sonthin'."

All three of us roared with more laughter.

"Really! And he had the nerve to try to holler at me looking like a hot mess. It's not like I'm *stuck up* or anything, but come on!"

The laughter came to a sudden stop at my last statement. Both women, mouths still open, raised their eyebrows, looked at each other, then back at me, and commenced to laugh even harder than before.

"Whatever! Forget both of you bitches!" I retorted.

Despite my best efforts, I was unable to keep myself from joining in. My mood significantly lightened, I grabbed a seat between my sisters, took my place in our little circle of healing, and eased my way back to life.

"Love can really fuck you up sometimes."
Nia

Chapter 8
Jasmine

The club was packed. So many souls crowded together at once, each with their own agenda.

My attention to the current conversation wavered as my imagination took over. I wondered what the story was behind the men and women masked by false pretenses, soaked in alcohol, and covered in their Friday's best.

This tall brother in a linen suit caught my eye. Its color, beige, complimented his chocolate skin. Face, shaved clean. Hair, neatly twisted in individuals. Nails, clean and trimmed. He smiled as he chatted with the pretty, younger girl in front of him – apparently, deeply enthralled with his own conversation. Did he have a woman at home? A wife and kids? Was he on the down-low, trying to conquer as many beautiful women as possible to fend off the burning desire for male companionship? Build his dwindling self esteem with as many women as possible?

A group of girls stood to the left of him. The one on the right of the group, consuming more drinks than she probably should. Her obnoxious presence was obvious from across the room. Her balance was unsteady. She spoke with loud gestures of her hands. Her words were indiscernible to me over the music and distance, but the effect they had was pretty clear. People across the bar occasionally stopped their conversation to glance at her and shake their heads— either in disgust or pity.

The "DL" brother on the right shot her an annoyed look over his shoulder after she pantomimed wildly and bumped his arm; the spilled contents of his drink staining the pant leg of his linen suit dark.

Trey Songz started over the system and Drunk-girl lost another piece of dignity. Though a decent lip-reader, I didn't need any special skills to understand that she was yelling "Ooooo, That's my shit!" She then, in typical drunken form, began to jam all by herself. She turned around and freaked the bar. Her dancing suggested she preferred a pole to the bar.

Was this an unusual side of her? Was she dealing with a recent loss – a bad breakup or the death of a loved one – by drowning her sorrows in liquor?

The irritated looks and the eye-rolls of her friends coupled with the way they tried to carry on their conversations while ignoring her antics, suggested this was a weekly ritual.

Maybe, she had demons from her childhood that she kept at bay by partying way too hard. Or, maybe the problem started before she was born? Alcoholism? Chickens coming home to roost through genetics?

Whatever the reason, she was making a fool out of herself. I wondered how she would feel in the morning. Would someone be home to shake their head at her as she vomited in the bathroom, hands hugging the porcelain god for dear life? She probably had a professional job to return to on Monday. One where she had to put on a front and a smile in order to numbly get through the rat-race and make it to another Friday Happy Hour.

So many lives. So many stories.

I love to try to read into folks, but wish I could apply it in my own life's story.

"You're such a dreamer, Jaz. You see all kinds of possibilities in life. You have so much hope. Teaching is more than your major. It's your calling."

I thought about what my dad told me in college. I had called him one day, doubting my decision to choose teaching over engineering, and he gave me those words of confidence. He always had faith in me. He gave me guidance in a strong, but empowering way.

Married in their teens and divorced in their twenties, my parents remained close when it came to raising their only child together. Everyone was impressed at how two parents managed to stay mature despite the weight that was placed on their heads at such an early age. Parents by 18-years-old, their parents, both deeply religious couples, encouraged them to do the right thing, as they had always done, and led them to marry. My parents continued to do the right thing, even after their union dissolved, by raising me in a loving, peaceful environment. Their past mistakes never stopped them from obtaining their dreams. It just gave them a harder road to travel.

"Let me make one thing very clear," my dad clarified to me one day, when I was old enough to use my age to figure out his own age when I was born. "Our mistake wasn't having you. It was taking on the responsibility of sex too early to handle it. You were the blessing despite our sins. You are our redemption. Doing right by you, no matter how hard it's been, has allowed us to be blessed. You were in the plans of the Almighty before even I was born. Baby, you were never a mistake."

Such wisdom and responsibility from a man so young. He would put some of these so-called "fathers" to shame. So many aren't even involved in the lives of my students. Of the ones I actually do see, the ignorance coming from some of their mouths leave little doubt as to why these kids have disciplinary and learning problems.

"Is that chick actually working the bar?" Nia said, referring to Drunk-girl.

My thoughts broken, *"You're such a dreamer, Jaz,"* I said to myself. I left the mental rooms of my mind and joined my friends in the real world.

"Damn, how drunk is she?" Nia looked on in disgust.

"Pretty damn drunk! Where does she think she is? The Stadium?"

"And what the hell do you know about the Stadium, Taz, you sneaky little heifer?"

"Uh, hello, Nia? You know some of our patient clientele. Some of them actually strip there."

"Anyway, girl, speaking of drunk, why was my baby sister so drunk when she came home from the club, she took a shit right on the walkway in the front yard? Not even the grass, right on the concrete. And homegirl didn't take a cute little poop in the yard, either. She took a massive, truck-driver, toilet-clogging dump right in front of my mom's porch. I went there to pick up some mail, and I saw it. I thought a Saint Bernard had gotten loose in the neighborhood or something."

I covered my mouth to hold in my laugh and keep from spitting my apple martini on the floor."

"Okay, what level of drunk is that? How drunk do you have to be to defecate in front of your own home?"

"Defecate, Dr. Vernan?" I interrupted teasing Taz.

She narrowed her hazel eyes in my direction at my sarcasm.

"Eliminate her bowels. Will that suffice?"

"Drunk enough that you do it in front of your date, who is dropping you off home. Aaand, this was the first time they went out."

"I guess that was the last time she saw him again. I bet he couldn't back up out of that driveway quick enough."

"That's just it. He called her the next day to go out again."

"Ewww! Men are nasty!" I said in disgust.

Taz raised her eyebrow at me. "Wait a minute, Nikia takes a dump in her front yard, while some guy is sitting there in his car, and you're calling *him* nasty? Please, explain."

"At least she was drunk. Hey, when you gotta go, you gotta go. But for him to see some girl's ass, who he barely knows, with shit coming from it, and still try to holler the very next day, you're nasty. Let some bamma take a shit in front of me, and see if I call his ass ever again. Shoot, I don't even want him taking a dump in the bathroom when we're together until at least six months of dating. He better hold it in until he's alone."

Nia had to put her drink down to that one. She was laughing at me so hard.

"Girl, you're sick. Your morals are jacked up. Let me find out you'll penalize a man for going number 2 too soon in the relationship. But hell, if it was Curtis, you'd probably be so far in the toilet, you'd know what he ate for breakfast."

Taz's eyes opened wide when she realized where Nia's joke went. My hurt expression stopped the laughing dead in its tracks. She hit too close to home. The truth in that statement made me realize just how much of a fool I'd been. Much like Drunk-girl, I've made myself look like an idiot while thinking I was having a good time. Nia's words slowed me, but I didn't falter. Something in me turned that shame and sadness to anger. At myself. At Curt.

"You're right. I was so far gone, I didn't care how much his shit stank. As long as he was shitting at my house."

Taz leaned forward in her chair and stared directly in my face. She looked at me with so much intensity that it threw me off for a second.

"He wasn't shitting at your house, sweetie, he was shitting on it," Taz said with no anger in her voice. Just clarity. She seized the moment and used it to break through to me. She realized I was having a breakthrough of my own.

"He's been shitting on my house – on me – for so long...I can't believe I've allowed him to do it."

I could taste the salt in the back of my sinuses as tears began to form. But I refused to let them fall. My will was strong. These were not tears born of sadness, but of anger, and they quickly evaporated under the heat of my emotions.

I grew up with the example of a true man. My father equipped me with all the tools I needed to function on my own on in a relationship. He wasn't abusive. He wasn't neglectful. He wasn't absent. He showed me as well as told me what to look for in a man, but the thing I was attached to was nowhere near his definition.

"What the fuck is wrong with me?" I said out loud, to myself more so than anyone else.

"You're just in love," Nia said; sadness and understanding in her voice. "Love can really fuck you up sometimes." She stared past me as she said that. Her own demons coming to the surface.

"Whatever, Jasmine! We're not going to let him screw your night up any more than he has. You are too beautiful and there are too many fine men available. If he can't get with the program, fuck him!" Taz said, uncharacteristically.

"Fuck him!" Nia agreed.

"Fuck him," I said.

Somewhere is the deepest recesses of my mind, a memory I had buried resurrected itself. I remembered the day of my graduation.

Time spent with Curt was sporadic and unpredictable. We never went out anymore, at least not off campus. For the most part, we spent time in my room, ordering food, watching movies, and having sex. He often cancelled our "dates" by just not showing up – no call, no nothing. The time we spent together, I was so happy, I was almost delirious. I couldn't do enough to please him. But when he wasn't with me, and I had no idea when or if I would see him again, I was so low it was pathetic. All I could do was wrap myself in my school work to keep from falling in a deep depression. My happiness centered around him.

I didn't want any bad feelings when we were together, so I stopped voicing any issues I had with him. I didn't want him to get mad and possibly leave early, so I made myself happy with the state of our relationship.

I stopped asking questions about his whereabouts. The lies were getting harder to believe anyway, so rather than shatter my illusion of him, I kept quiet.

I stopped asking to meet his mother. He stopped making excuses to why she wasn't available. Eventually, we both just acted like I never asked.

I stopped sharing just how bad things were with my friends; uncomfortable with their criticism of him. I felt like a closet drug addict, withdrawing from the world to hide my shame.

My graduation, the day that all of my hard work and dedication was to be rewarded with a degree from the university, came. More importantly, it was the day that Curtis would finally meet my family.

He had known about the graduation ceremony and dinner for at least two months. Curtis gassed my head up with how proud he was and how good I was going to look in my cap and gown. He even talked about the gray suit he bought just for my special occasion. This situation was too special to even consider him standing me up. This wasn't just a date; it was a life event. A graduation.

A graduation that came and went without so much as a phone call. My parents bought my lie that Curt couldn't get out of work and would be there for dinner. After I had spent most of my dinner celebration at Houston's barely touching my food and alternating between glancing at my cell phone and glancing at the door, my parents knew better. They gave each other knowing glances and silent exchanges all night.

"So, Jaz, you're going to be teaching at you're old high school? That's going to be weird, huh? You're not that much older than the students. Hmmmph! A few of the people you went to school with might even still be there. I know that Lewis boy still is," she laughed. At 39, my mother still looked close to my age. She looked like a thicker version of Salli Richardson in Low Down Dirty Shame. Her skin as smooth as it was in the pictures of her holding me as a baby. Jet black hair showing no gray. She got more play from guys my age than I did.

"Come on now, Aiyanna, the boy was stupid, but he wasn't that stupid. Besides, if you haven't graduated after a certain age, I think they just mail the test for the GED to your house." They both laughed.

My parents had such a beautiful relationship. Everyone who knows them say they've never seen two exes get along so well. They look so happy around each other that everyone who doesn't know them naturally assumes they're together. I know my dad wishes they still were. He never forgave himself for cheating on my mom. My mom was and is a strong woman, and she wasn't having that. Not while she was still working, going to college, raising a baby and being a loving and supportive wife. She once told me that she forgave him, but she couldn't forget. The feelings just weren't there after that. She also admitted that she could handle having a child at that age, but having a husband was much harder. It was easy to control your little child, but a big kid who thought he knew everything—that was more stressful. His cheating was as good an excuse as any to get out of the marriage. I think she had been so sheltered by her strict, religious parents that she wanted to live her life for a little while without someone else telling her what to do.

I looked at my dad and wondered why my mom didn't run at the chance to get back with him. From the time I was a little girl, my friends always told me how cute my dad was. When they played MASH, my dad would frequently be named as one of the men to marry—if fate and your favorite number chose so. I never understood how my dad could rank up there with the likes of Tevin Campbell and Christopher Williams. It would gross me out to no end, but it would never stop the giggles and the crushes. Five-foot-nine with smooth cocoa-brown skin, clean-cut hair, mustache and goatee, and a beautiful smile, a lot of people say my dad resembles Larenz Tate. I never saw it, but the moment someone did mention it, I could never look at Larenz Tate the same.

Everyone wanted to come to my birthday parties not because I was that popular, but because my dad would be there. He would come to every birthday to help out. My parents were so close that my mom would let him bring his girlfriend, if he had one at the time. He would only bring a woman around me if he was serious about her. So far, I've only met three. I know at least one of them that couldn't handle how close my parents were. Even though there was never anything going on after the divorce, I think she knew he still was in love with his ex. It was the eyes. You could always tell by how the hardness in them softened when he looked at her. My mom is no angel, but he thinks of her as one.

He looks more his age than she, but he still looks good. A little gray at the temples and a few lines in the corners of his eyes when he laughs, but my dad was and is still a handsome man.

At dinner, I looked at my dad looking at my mom, and felt envy. He still held so much love in his eyes for her.

"Baby, where is this Curtis boy?" After she had dispensed with the formalities, she went straight into business mode. "I thought you said he would be here for dinner. I have yet to meet this boy after almost 3 years, and I thought today would be the day. What could he poss—"

"I know, Mama," I cut her off before she could get started. "He gets caught up at work, a lot. Sometimes, they have to do mandatory overtime. Maybe tomorrow..." Tears threatened to overtake me. Besides the thought of being stood up on my graduation day, the disapproval in my mother's eyes made me want to fall into pieces. She was as strong as she was beautiful. She knew how to cut through the bullshit, and I couldn't hold up the lie much longer.

Though she kept her voice low, the anger in it was palpable. "Work is work, but this graduation day has been a long time coming. He had enough advance notice to request off. That's no excuse for..."

"Sweetie, let's not talk about this right now. This is supposed to be a happy day for our daughter. We can talk about this *boy* later. Tonight, it's about Jasmine." Daddy stepped in to rescue me from full disclosure and final humiliation. He was the cooling Pisces water to her searing Leo fire. My mom opened her mouth to speak again, and he gently touched the back of her hand. My dad learned a long time ago not to fight fire with fire when it comes to her. She was the queen of confrontation; getting loud and angry only fueled her into a frenzy. You'd come out from her verbal lashing trying to pick up the pieces of your dignity that was shattered. When she was right, nothing could stop her in an argument. And tonight, she was right. It just wasn't the right time. My dad gently let her know that through a light touch and a calm voice.

She backed down.

"Okay, Michael. You're right. It's about mytonight."

"Our baby," he corrected.

A smile of gratitude graced my face as I looked at Daddy.

"So, have you thought about what you want for your graduation present?" My dad smiled right back at me and all was well for the moment. My mother looked back and forth between the two of us, unhappy that she didn't get to speak her mind, but satisfied that holding her tongue was the right thing to do.

The rest of the dinner went a lot smoother. Eating and laughing with my folks helped to ease the pain of being stood up – yet, again. All of a sudden, I saw this angry short woman sprinting in our direction.

"Hi, Mr. Lee. Hi, Ms. Saddlewhite-Lee." (My mom never changed her married name.)

It was Nia. She came barreling towards our table and stopped right behind my seat.

"Uh, I know you guys were eating, but this is a real emergency. Could I borrow Jasmine for a few minutes?"

"How are you doing, Nia?   How's your mom?"

My mom didn't care how much of an emergency it was, she was always a stickler for manners. She would never put up with rudeness under any circumstances.

"Oh, I'm sorry, Ms. S. I'm fine. My mom's doing good.   She just got over bronchitis, but she's good." Nia rushed through the formalities to appease my mother.

"That's good. Tell her I said hi, and I still have her..."

My dad cut her off. "Sweetie, what did you come all the way here for?"

All of a sudden, Taz came speed-walking to the table. Her face was slightly red, and she looked like she was in a hurry. She composed herself at the last minute.

"Hi, Mom. Hi, Dad." She leaned over and gave them each a kiss and a hug. "Actually, we were already in the area at White Flint Mall. I didn't have my cell phone, and I knew you guys were eating here." She turned to speak to me. "We were trying to catch you before you left to see if you wanted to go to Dave and Busters." Dave and Busters was like a Chuck E. Cheese for grownups. You played games, you won tickets, and you cashed them in for real prizes – like a TV – if you had enough.

"Well, we were just about to pay the bill. Go on, Jasmine, your mom and I will be all right."

"No, I'll stay with you guys. We can go..."

"Go on, Jaz. You need to get out with your friends." My mom said it like there was no choice in the matter.

I really didn't feel like going, but for some reason, I could tell there was more to the story and the curiosity was motivating my depressed body.

"Okay, Mommy. I'll call you when I get home." I leaned in and kissed her, then my dad.

"Okay, baby. We'll talk later."

She raised her thick eyebrows as she spoke. I knew what that meant.

On the way to the car, Nia was walking fast and hard. She was way ahead of Taz and I, and it seemed like she was furious about something. Taz walked with me, but she wouldn't look at me.

"What's going on with you two?"

Nobody spoke until we were in the car.

"Why are we going to Dave and Buster's?" I tried again. The silent treatment was worrying me.

"Because Curt is there," Taz finally said.

"Curt? What the fuck is he doing there?"

"Apparently, it must be Family Day," Nia said without looking back at me. She glanced over to her left, turned on her turn signal, and merged over.

"What does that mean? Are you sure? He's supposed to be with me!" My mind wouldn't process what they just told me.

"We're sure. We saw him go in with a woman and two little kids, so we followed them. They were his kids, Jasmine, and that was definitely his wife, or woman, or whatever."

"But, he doesn't have any kids. He has a nephew by his brother, but..." All of a sudden, tears began to rise as the realization started to sink in.

"No, don't you dare! Don't cry for that motherfucker! He doesn't deserve any tears from you. I'm going to call my cousin to come out here and bang the shit out of him. I told you he was no good, Jaz. His fucking-ass…"

Nia was on fire. A true Libran with a little Scorpio from her late October birthday, she didn't like for anyone to be fucked over – unless she was the one doing the fucking.

"Not now, Niani. She doesn't need 'I told you so's'. She's already upset. Let her see for herself and then, we can talk." Always the voice of reason, Taz was another Libran, but born earlier in the month. She possessed more diplomacy skills and less manipulative ways. Both had a need for balance, harmony, and justice. Both were social leaders and very perceptive of people. They knew how to work a room. They also knew who to keep your eye on and could spot a fake bitch a mile away.

We pulled into the parking lot of D&B. There wasn't much of a line to get in yet, but come 10pm, there would be. Nia walked ahead as usual, scanning the room for Curtis and his brood.

I saw them before anyone else did.

There he was. The man I loved. The man I wanted to bear children for, sitting there laughing – that sexy smile of his – with kids of his own.

I couldn't believe it! Nausea stole my breath as a sick feeling shot through my stomach and settled hard. My heart felt like it was being crushed. The ache, too painful for words. Vomit threatened—no demanded—to come up my dry esophagus. My only strength was the thought that if I vomited in this place, it would cause a scene. Everyone would look in my direction, including him. I didn't want him to see me. I didn't want anyone to see me.

I wanted to be invisible.

So many emotions were competing for my

attention: anger, hurt, humiliation, shock. Even relief. So many things made sense now. How I could have been so blind, I didn't know.

His two children were gorgeous. The little girl had her dad's light brown complexion and light-colored hair. Two short ponytails, each on one side of her head. A cherubim's smile complimented with dimples and one missing tooth. She looked about five.

The little boy, who looked about two or three, sat on his daddy's lap. A powder blue kid's Ralph Lauren polo shirt. Jean shorts. Little Jordan's. He was the exact replica of his dad, but just a little darker – a beautiful shade of honey– with black curly hair. Looking at him sent a sharp pang through my palpitating heart. That's exactly how I thought our child would look.

The wife/babymama was caramel-brown and cute. Dark brown, almost black, long hair. Shapely Thick – like Raven Simone's size, with the breasts to match. When she smiled at him, anger caused the air around me to heat up. She resembled me in the face.

Out the corner of my tear-filled eyes, I saw Nia, red-faced, take a couple of steps in his direction. My hand shot out and grabbed her by her little arm. I couldn't talk, but my eyes pleaded with her as my head frantically shook "no."

"Fuck that, Jaz! We're going over there and blowing him the fuck up. I'm telling everything! I've got dates, locations...Aw, hell, naw! That nigga is going to get the shock of his life!" Nia was in a rage. The DC ghetto-side was coming out of her. I've seen her like this before and knew that I'd never be able to talk her out of it.

What could I say? I felt so stupid that I couldn't talk. What if his girl got indignant and got in Nia's face? She would have had to get her ass kicked with the mood that Nia was in. I might even take some of my hurt out on her. Except, I couldn't! It wasn't her fault. And there were kids there. I didn't want to cause any of them grief. Only Curtis.

"Worse than all of that," I thought, *"what if he denies everything?"* What if he looks at me like I was trash and accuses me of being crazy. What if he starts yelling and cursing and talking to me like he didn't know me – like he never told me he loved me too many times to count – all in an effort to save face in front of his family? What if he denied me? I couldn't take that.

That would hurt beyond imagination.

I looked at Taz—my eyes my only form of communication—pleading with her to intervene. Reading my thoughts, Taz grabbed Nia's other arm, and they both started arguing.

The commotion caused Curt to look in our direction. He stopped saying whatever he was saying mid-sentence and all the color drained from his face. Wifey took note of his changed expression and followed his eyes. She saw my girls arguing, one trying to pull away, and the other holding on very tightly. Behind those two, in the middle of it all, she noticed me. Our eyes locked and something passed between us. I didn't know if it was recognition or what, but something shown in her eyes. Maybe, it was the way I looked at her, then Curt, then back to her, with grief in my eyes. I didn't know.

Curt dropped the fork he was holding. It made a loud crash as it hit his plate and then fell under the table. He clumsily reached under trying to get it, practically pushing his son off his lap. Wifey looked back in his direction confused and suspicious. The fork obviously wasn't that important. It looked like he was hiding.

Another emotion took over.

Disgust.

I couldn't stand another minute of this. I grabbed Nia, turned her in my direction, and let out a choked and pathetic "Please."

Nia finally saw the hurt in my eyes and agreed to go. But not without first shooting a hateful look in their direction (for what seemed like an eternity) and shaking her head. We headed out of D&B (Nia leading the way, marching like Ms Sophia from The Color Purple) and left Curtis to live out the life he already had with someone else. The dream I had of a life with him shattered and crumbled with each somber step.

Particles slowly released into to the wind.

A noise at the bar caught my attention and interrupted my trip to "Bad Memories Land." Drunk-girl had popped her back a little too hard and the serious junk in her ample trunk knocked a plate off the bar. She stopped her show to turn around and assess the damage. Ketchup was smeared down the bottom of her tight, white dress, making it look like she started her period. One French fry stuck right between the imprint of her crack. She was stumbling. Sweaty. Pieces of her real hair frizzed out of the bad weave-job. Drunk-girl's friends just started to walk away to stairs leading to the 2nd level – leaving her alone with the wolves. The whole scene was embarrassing – even more so because she had no clue. When she bent over to pick up the plate, men still gawked at her ass. The guy next to her even plucked the French fry off and ate it. The brother next to him gave him dap for his comedic display of boldness. The same guy tried to push up on Drunk-girl while she was barely able to stand. Hoping she would prove herself to be an easy lay. No shame. Disgusting.

Sometimes, men make me sick to my stomach.

"I want you to cum for me, babygirl."
Cameron

Chapter 9:
Niani

Looking at that drunk-ass, chicken-head broad was pissing me off! Why did sisters have to degrade themselves like that? Bad enough that her white dress was so thin and tight, you could not only see the triangle of her pink thong in the front, but you could see the dimples of her cheeks in the back. Her ass looked like a Chinese checkerboard. The French fry and ketchup actually helped by taking attention away from that cellulite-ridden donkey of hers. And did that nigga just eat the fry that was stuck to her ass?

I wrinkled my nose and leaned over to speak. "Bet you that French fry smells like booty sweat," I said.

Jasmine and Tazanna burst out laughing. I must have said it pretty loud because the three girls and one guy standing close to our miniVIP section laughed, too.

This night was what I needed. I was starting to feel better. Cameron hadn't even entered my mind.

"*Damn!*" I thought to myself, "*He just did.*"

This was becoming one of the hardest

things I've ever had to do.   Thank God, James was out of town, so I could relax a little and stop pretending I was happy all the time.

Right away, I regretted that thought.

If he were home more often, this probably would never have happened.   At least, forgetting about Cameron wouldn't be as painful.   It was easier to not think about Cameron while staring at James' dimples.

There were so many things I loved about him.   His laugh.   The way he smiled and touched the front of his teeth with his tongue when he had something dirty on his mind.   The way he closed his eyes and bit his lip when I rode him and dug my nails into his flexed six-pack.   After all these years, I still hate to admit how fine he is.

Though Cameron has him beat by four inches in height (and and maybe 3 inches dick-length), he definitely beats Cameron in the looks department.

"Still, there's something about Cameron that I can't shake."

"You getting another Mai Tai, Niani?"   Taz was being unusually liberal with the alcohol to-night.   She ordered another shot of Remy for her-self and one for Jaz.   Jaz opened her mouth to protest, but thought better of it and closed it.

"Let me finish the one I have, first."   I was babysitting my second drink and wasn't sure I needed a third.

As pretty as James was, he wasn't afraid to work hard.   That's one of the things I love about him.   It's also one of the things I hate.   The store in Jersey is getting more business, and before this trip, he had been there just about every weekend.   He'll be there until he can hire a new manager.   Since his other cousin, Deon, was locked up, he hasn't found anyone he can trust. Building a small fortune with his clothing store, barbershops, and laundromat takes sacrifice. His hard work comes at a price – our relationship. Second place is where I stand most times when it comes to his work, and I was never one to take a backseat to anything. Maybe, that's how Cameron came into the picture?

That's not entirely true. Men approach me all the time, but before Cameron, I never paid them much attention. I don't know what it was about him. The day we met, I wasn't in the market for cheating. In fact, I had never cheated on anyone before. It just happened:

"If you need some help, I could pick you up; just to help you see the screen better."

I was at the movie ticket kiosk in Arundel Mills Mall. I was trying to purchase tickets when I was interrupted by the deep voice of a stranger, who made a joke about my height. Bad move. I turned around and mugged this dude behind me – looked him up and down. With a roll of my eyes and a suck of my pearly whites, I turned back around; I didn't say a word.

He chuckled, but persisted.

"I apologize. That was my lame attempt at initiating a conversation with a very pretty girl. Don't take offense. I really meant it as a compliment. I love your height."

Again, I turned around, mugged him hard, and looked him up and down; but this time I spoke.

"And, why is that, Shaq?" At first glance, he was all right looking.

He laughed again. A deep, easy laugh. He wasn't getting the picture no matter how hard I tried.

"I just think short women – my bad – vertically-challenged women are so sexy. "

I gave up a little smile and he seemed to be encouraged.

As I said before, at first glance, he looked all right, but the longer I looked at him, the more attractive he became.

"Let's just ignore my lame first attempt and start over. I'm Cameron."

I smiled, but didn't offer my name.

"So you're going to the movies?"

"No, I just like to peruse the ticket kiosks just for fun. Actually going to the movies is waaaay too exciting." My sarcasm index was high.

"Ummm, have you ever heard of the word rhetorical?" His smile never wavered.

"Touchè, my dark one," I thought. He could take what I gave and dish it out as well.

Something about him was holding my attention. I didn't know if it was that crooked smile of his or his easy-going demeanor. Maybe it was his cockiness. Maybe it was his eyes. Slightly Asian, almost black eyes set against dark chocolate skin.

I turned back around at the kiosk. Lack of a timely selection caused it to kick me back to the beginning.

"Great! Now, I have to start over."

"Sorry about that."

I turned back to this deep-voiced stranger. He was still smiling. Smiling hard, in fact.

In spite of myself, I was beginning to warm up to him. Trying to rectify this feeling, I looked him up and down with a frown. He just smiled harder.

"You're not from DC are you?"

"Why do you say that? I can't be from DC?"

"Not with that bright-ass orange Roca Wear shirt you have on, you can't."

His smile faded. That wasn't the reaction he was going for when he looked in his closet that morning.

"Actually, I'm from the city. Baltimore city, born and raised."

"Well, that explains a lot," I smirked.

"Let's not get into the whole Baltimore-DC thing. If we do, I'll have to mention that your people still wear slouch socks."

I laughed a little. "Slouch socks are so '97." If you were brave enough to visit, you would see that."

"Well, I patrol enough ghettos in my own city, so you can keep your Southeast."

"Patrol? What do you do?"

"I'm a police officer."

"*A cop,*" I thought. "*Interesting.*"

"So are you here with your man?"

"*And here it comes,*" I thought.

"Actually, I'm here with my girls." Jaz and, Chanté, another mutual friend, were going with me to see "The Hangover."

"So, you don't have a man?" He said hopefully.

"Sorry, but I do." His disappointment was visible. "He's at home where all men should be – out of the way and out of trouble."

His laugh reached me in a different way and I was getting warm.

"Well, no offense to him, but I have to say that you are a very beautiful woman. Feisty, too. I'm sure he's got his hands full. I hope he can handle it all."

"He hasn't had any problem handling it for the past six years." A little defensive tone in my voice caused him to back down. He smiled apologetically.

"Ummm, I'm sorry I took up so much of your time, so I'll let you get back to the kiosk. I don't want to make you miss your movie."

"Okay. It was nice meeting you...Cameron, is it?"

"Yes, Sweetheart, Cameron. And, it was nice meeting you Miss 'I don't give my name out to strange, tall men'. I saw that look on your face when I introduced myself."

I laughed.

"It's Niani."

He stopped for a second as if I caught him off guard.

"That's a beautiful name. I'm sorry. It's just that I thought you would have some ghetto name like Tremaine or Capricia. What does it mean?"

"It means 'WIC vouchers on the fifth' in Yoruba."

His laughter was infectious. Something passed between us.

"Actually, it doesn't mean anything. My mom was just hood-classy."

"Well, it's still beautiful, just like you."

We stared at each other for a few seconds. "Look, I don't want to step on anyone's toes, but I really would like to get to know you, even just as a friend. I don't know what it is, but I never met a girl like you."

This sounded so much like a line I said, "Wait a minute. How old are you?"

"Twenty-four."

My nose wrinkled. I didn't do younger men.

"What was that?" .

"I'm sorry. I just don't like to talk to younger men."

"Younger? Wait...How old are you?"

"How old do I look?"

"Twenty."

"Try twenty-eight, young buck."

"For real? Okay, I'm not going to get into the whole 'age-ain't-nothing-but-a-number' thing, but if it's only for friendship, what harm could it be to take my number?"

I really wasn't interested after I heard his age, so I turned back to the kiosk and ordered my ticket.

But, he didn't give up that easily.

"So, are you going to take my number?"

I figured I'd let him have this little victory – even if I planned to erase his number out of my phone afterwards.

We were at a crossroads. My plan was already decided, but I looked at him and said nothing for a few seconds for effect – dramatic pause. Then, I pulled my phone out.

"Okay, give me your number."

I entered his contact info and pressed save – still wondering whether it was a good idea. As hard as I tried not to, I was really feeling him.

"Are you going to give me your number?"

My eyes passed over his form once more – this time in pleasant appraisal of it. With a mischievous smile, I shook my head and started walking away. I looked back as I said, "I've got a man, remember."

He stared back with a serious look on his face, nodding slowly, as if silently consenting to the challenge.

That was over a year ago. I don't know why I never erased his number. I don't why I called him that first time. I don't know why I went out with him the next week to the Baltimore Aquarium. I don't know why I rode with him on duty the week after that. I definitely don't know why I let him make love to me later that night (on a smoldering summer evening, in front of his fireplace lit for effect – not warmth). All I know is that it's been a year, and I'm slowly purging him out of my system. Been a hell of a time doing it, but I'm starting to see some light.

"So, are you really done with him?" Jasmine asked timidly—almost whispering—as if the sound of her voice could limit the pain she might cause.

"I have to be. I can't keep doing this. It's too much. My feelings for him are too...too strong. I love James...and lying to him has been killing me." I took a deep breath. "The sad part is that the more I lie, the easier it gets, and the better I get at it."

"Good!" Taz chimed. "James is a good man. He's been nothing but good to you, and, uh, you *are* supposed to get married next fall." Always the voice of reason, Taz had a way of bringing me back to reality.

"I didn't plan for it to go this far. I mean, shit! I actually fell in love with him. And, I don't even know how it happened. That shit sneaks up on you, you know."

"I know," Taz said empathetically. "Trust me. Once you start an addiction, it's hard to let it go."

"What do you know about addictions?

You've never had a bad habit in your life! You don't even drink coffee. You've damn sure never been addicted to a man. I've seen you in action. Hmmmph! Please! If they don't act right, it's over. "Take 'em or leave 'em" Taz."

Taz smiled weakly at Jasmine's compliments but never responded. She seemed distracted. Sad, even. Then, she noticed me looking at her, and all doubt left her face. Without warning, a mask of confidence replaced her countenance. She looked as if nothing was on her mind.

But for a second...

Who could ever tell what she was thinking? Always hard to read, Taz could be a cold person on the best of days – at least, with her own feelings. Like a Vulcan, she carried on day-to-day decisions with minimal emotion and maximal logic.

I looked down at my espadrilles, trying to avoid her eyes. She's so private; I rarely pry into her life. Only if she volunteers, do I get nosy. She rarely seeks anybody's help for any issues. It's always the other way around.

I glanced at the bar. That drunk chick was nowhere to be found. Must have left with the dude trying to push up on her. Suddenly, thoughts of him and his friends running a train on her in the bathroom had my stomach turning and my conscience nagging. There, but for the grace of God, go I. A quick prayer that she was in the safe company of her friends and then, my thoughts returned to Cameron.

A little more time, and I could get through this. I just needed to keep my distance, which was easier now that he stopped calling me. Easier and harder at the same time.

Out of everything, I think I missed his

phone calls the most.   The calls during work-time to make me laugh. The calls late at night to tell me that he missed me. I had to keep my phone hidden or on silent, most of the time, when I stayed with James. But when I stayed at my apartment, those nights that we talked were the best. There wasn't that sense of urgency that we had when we were physically together. Always aware of the time. Always having to get back before I was missed. When we were on the phone and I was home, the night was ours.

James always wanted me to move into his house with him, but I never wanted to feel like I was dependent on a man. He made so much more than me, refused to let me pay for anything when we went out, and took me on exotic and elaborate trips that I could never afford. My friends thought I was crazy, but I had to assert my independence somehow.

Before Cameron, I missed James most nights when I went home alone, but my stubbornness would never let me admit it. It gave me a sense of accomplishment despite my loneliness, to have a place of my own. But, when I started seeing Cameron, I was glad I kept my apartment for another reason. Privacy.

Too scared to let Cameron actually come there, I would call as soon as I got home. We shared so much in our conversations. Our dreams. Our insecurities. Our best and worst moments. I got to see some parts of him that he rarely showed.

And the phone sex, something I had never done before, was off the chain. His deep voice over fiber optics sending chills through my body and coaching me to orgasm: "I want you to cum for me, babygirl." Hearing him moaning on the other end always made me ache to be filled with his thickness.

Sweet torture.

The best part about our phone dates was talking to him until the sun came up. Or, better yet, talking so long, we fell asleep on each other. Mornings, I would wake up, and he would still be asleep on the other end. I would press buttons on the phone to wake him up for work. Some-times, I would wake up during the night and still hear him lightly snoring on the other end. In the curtain of darkness, I would try to pretend he was right next to me sleeping. Those nights made it feel like it was real. There was no doubt it was temporary, but it was a peace with him that I didn't have on the regular.

But, all of that was over now. It had to be. Somebody was going to get emotionally hurt if I kept this up. Maybe, physically hurt. Maybe, killed. Maybe, all three. And the most important part was that somebody might be me. I had to let it go.

"I think your phone is ringing."

Jasmine caught my attention and brought me back. I was so deep in thought, I didn't notice that Taz was talking to someone. One of her col-leagues. I've seen her in the office a few times. Pretty woman with huge breasts and a perfect lit-tle body. Sickening. She was cool the times I met her, though. Not stuck up like some doctors. In-sisted I call her Corrine – not Dr. So-and-so. And, I loved her cinnamon and gold locks. They were so perfect. One of the reasons I chose to cut my hair and go natural. (After realizing how much maintenance was needed to keep them looking good, I let go of the idea of having locks.) The woman was dressed to the nines tonight.

Men were practically drooling.

She glanced at me, smiled, and waved. I waved back. Taz looked back at me, then to the ground. Now, she did look nervous. *"What was that?"*

"Uh, your phone?" Jaz leaned into my line of vision to get my attention.

"Oh."

The music couldn't be heard in the club, but the light angrily flashed in my Coach bag. I fumbled through the hot mess in my purse to get to it, my Mac Lip Glass coming out with the phone and falling on the floor.

It was Cameron. I answered on reflex, forgetting that I was trying to avoid him.

"Hello?"

Silence on the other end. Then a ragged breath.

"Hello?" I repeated, straining to hear over the music.

"Nia? I didn't think you would..."

"Wait, I can barely hear you. Give me a sec."

I maneuvered to the back to get to the bathroom and away from the music. More people packed the place by the second. One eager patron grabbed my hand on the way. I yanked it back without looking up. Squeezing my way through, I made it to the Ladies' room, which seemed like it had its own club going on.

"Go ahead, Cam. I can hear you." I tried to make my voice sound cold.

"Kevin's dead." Then, he started to choke and sob.

"What? What? How did..."

"I should have been there...If I was...some dumb, skinny little kid, Nia!" A jumble of words between sobs. He sounded so broken. So lost.

"Baby, wait! I can't understand you. Calm down, please! Oh, God! I'm so sorry. Oh, God..."

"I need you. Please...I...need you. I can't..." His voiced croaked, and he couldn't finish his plea. His words tugged at my very being. It had been so long since I even spoke to him, but the feelings resurfaced instantly. What was I going to do?

"I'm coming. I'm in DC, but give me some time...I'm coming now, baby."

I hung up and rushed back to our section. Corrine was whispering something in Taz's ear. Jasmine looked bored. I rushed in the middle of them, almost tripping on the steps.

"I've gotta go!"

"What?" They both turned around and spoke simultaneously.

"I've gotta go! Cameron called. His partner was killed! I don't know what happened, but he needs me! I'm so sorry!"

"It's okay, Nia. We understand," Jaz said sympathetically and glanced back at Taz for consensus.

"Go. Call us when you get some details. Let us know you're all right." Taz was concerned, but she let me go without saying anything negative. Not even a word of caution. This was not the time to try to talk me out of seeing Cameron, and she knew it.

I left as fast as my little legs could carry me. Cutting in and out of the lanes on New York ave heading towards 295, I had one thing on my mind.

Cameron.

"I'll make sure she has a very good time with
me."
Corrine

Chapter 10
Tazanna

"What was she doing here?"
My heart felt like it wanted to jump out of
my chest when I saw her coming towards me.

She smiled as we made eye contact. Her
lips, painted a reddish plum, were moist. Inviting. With a wink, she ran her tongue over her
teeth. That wasn't a smile you give your homegirl. It seemed like the whole club saw us looking
at each other and could tell right off the bat. I felt
like I had a big sign on my forehead: "I like wom-
en!"

"What the hell is she doing here?"
Her tight black dress cut dangerously low
in the front. I couldn't see her feet, but I knew
she had to be wearing four-inch stilettos. Her
two-toned locks were freshly twisted and pinned.
A few loose ones framed her face. Huge, tear-
drop diamond earrings. Eyes, smoky shadow on
her hazelnut complexion. A crowd of men parted
like the Red sea to allow her to pass. Men were
instinctively turning in her direction before they
saw her – as if they could smell sexiness oozing in
the room.

A tall, light-skinned brother stepped directly in her path.

She stopped and played the game of cat and mouse. I couldn't hear her words, but I could tell she was flirting. She kept glancing at me between words. She looked over his shoulder so much that even he glanced backwards.

"What the hell was she doing here?"

My feelings, torn between nervous anxiety and irritating jealousy, kept me fighting to keep my poker face on. I glanced at my friends, who were in their own mental worlds for the time being. Good. I was shook and they would know something was wrong.

Corrine looked at me once more, satisfied that she had got my attention, and then politely brushed him off. The guy was so impressed that he didn't even appear upset. He glanced at her backside as she walked away and rubbed his goatee – smiling as if he was satisfied with the brief opportunity to be graced with her presence. He should have been. It was much more than any other guy was getting.

"What's up, Chica?"

She came in our VIP and sat on the edge of my seat.

"Heeeyy…um, what are you doing here?" My tone came off more annoyed than surprised. I tried not to sound irritated. I wasn't sure if I was more bothered by her showing up uninvited or by her flirting in front of me.

"I just needed to get out. Man, it's been a rough week! I remembered you said you guys were meeting here tonight, so I figured I didn't have to hang out by myself – looking pathetic. I called to see if it was okay, but you didn't answer your phone. I decided to try my luck anyway."

I glanced at my phone. One missed call six minutes ago. She was already here. Too far to send her back home if I wanted to.

She leaned in and hugged me. I returned the hug and she whispered dangerously close to my ear.

"I had to see you tonight. Mmmm, you look so good."

I was still pissed that she showed up, but she was so close to my spot, the heat from her breath was making it hard to think. I was grateful for the darkness of the club. No one could see me blush. Instantly, I was turned on.

"Where's the hubby?" I pulled back breaking contact and trying to change the subject. "He didn't want to come out? I haven't seen him in a month of Sundays. How's he doing?"

She raised her eyebrows. "Oh, he's fine. Busy as ever. He's working on this big case, so he's been buried up to his ears in paperwork. Besides, who would be home with Jewel and Jade if he came with me?"

Jewel and Jade were her beautiful three-year-old twins. Aptly named for their green eyes. Corrine's husband, a fine specimen of a white man, passed some of his traits on to his girls. Hazel-green eyes. Dark, curly hair. He has a cool personality, too. They were a perfect match. If he ever consciously decided to pick chocolate in his life, then he picked the right one – Corrine was a bad sister. She picked a winner, too. Educated. Handsome. Doting father. Loving husband. Shoot, good credit. One thing about sisters, if they end up choosing white, most of them are going to pick a good one. Not some raggedy, sad thing to put on the arm just because – like some of our color-struck brothers have.

"*Ugh!   There I go again.   I need to get over that.*"

"The girls want to come over this weekend, too. All they talk about is Tori and Taylor. Those girls are going to work my nerves asking about them."

Tori, my bossy three-year-old , and Taylor, my quiet five-year-old . My little women, each a different side of my personality. Surrogate sisters to the twins. Thinking about my babies while I was out always brought a little stab of guilt. They should be deep in peaceful sleep right now.

Not stressed and confused like their mother is right now.

Being this close to Corrine was making me uncomfortable. I shifted in my chair, not sure of what to do next. I looked to Nia for a diversion, but she was already distracted – trying to talk on the phone in the midst of all this clamor. Before I could get her attention, she shot up and started walking to the back with the phone to her ear; probably, to get to somewhere a little less noisy.

I looked at Jasmine, but she was staring off into the crowd, deep in thought. Well, she was no help either.

Corrine saw another opportunity to be bold, and took it. She placed her hand on my knee as she leaned in.

"You know, if you drove by yourself, we can get a room after we leave here," she suggested. "I've been thinking about the last time in the parking lot. I really need to finish what you started. Wanting you is keeping me up at night. Sometimes, I'm jonesin' so bad, I have to make myself cum just to fall asleep. I need to taste you."

She was being so forward in public that it

was really beginning to irk me. The worst part was, even with how upset I was, I could still feel myself getting wet. Her leaning in this position gave me a perfect view of her cleavage. I struggled not to keep looking down.

I was so nervous that I began to perspire.

Her fingers touching the inside of my knee gave a light squeeze. My face got hot as I could feel myself blush. Partly from embarrassment and partly from anger. Her being so bold this close to my inner circle was beginning to turn me off. I pulled away and looked at her. I was two seconds telling her to back the fuck off, when Nia stumbled in front of us.

"I've gotta go!"

"What?" Jaz and I responded in unison.

She was frantic. I don't know why, but I knew it was about Cameron before she said anything. Words of protest began to form in my head, but when she said that his partner had been killed, I knew I couldn't think of anything to say that would change her mind. I left it alone. She's a big girl, and she should be allowed to make her own mistakes. Who was I to get on somebody about making decisions that made life more complicated? Especially, when mine was so fucked up.

I let her go.

After Niani left, I knew Jasmine would be next. After Nia's statement, she had been preoccupied for almost the last half hour. Her mood wasn't the same.

"Do you mind if I called it an early night? My sinuses are starting to bother me. I'm not feeling this whole scene anymore."

"I know. Girl, I just got here and the loud music is starting to give me a headache." Corrine was eager to change scenery also.

"It's okay, Jaz. It's getting a little late, even though we never got to the dance floor. Plus, you don't look like you're in the mood to hang out anymore. Go on home, girl."

"You sure? I mean, I know how much you wanted to hang tonight. I feel like I'm abandoning you."

"Oh don't you worry. I'll keep her company. I still have a lot of energy left."

I cringed. The double meaning was so obvious, my ears were burning. I just knew Jaz was going to ask her what she meant by it.

Instead, she remained oblivious. She even seemed relieved.

"Good! I know she'll still have a good time with you. I didn't want to ruin her night."

"Oh, I'll make sure she has a *very* good time with me. You go home and get some rest." She leaned over and hugged Jaz. We made eye contact and she winked. I gasped at her boldness and I looked away into the crowd.

"Don't look so disappointed," Jasmine said as she gave me a quick hug, "I'm leaving you in good hands."

If only she knew how good.

And I wasn't disappointed, I was nervous. I straightened my shoulders and forced myself to look relaxed and happy.

"I'm good, sweetie. You go on home. You guys can make this up to me later." This was enough to ease her guilt.

"Okay, I'm gone. I've got a few things I need to take care of."

"Bye, Jasmine," Corrine said, before she took a sip of my drink.

"Bye, Jaz. Call me later."

She left in such a hurry, she didn't respond. This night wasn't ending how I expected. *"I was trying so hard to be good,"* I thought, *"but I think someone in the universe wants me to slip up."*

Corrine looked down at me and extended her hand – the one with her wedding ring. Without thinking, I grabbed her back in kind.

She gently pulled me up to standing and said "Let's go. I have a few things I need to take care of, too."

Her lips parted and the small, pink tip of her tongue moistened them. A voice in the back of my mind said, *"Someone definitely wants you to slip up."*

"He did something so unlike him..."
Nia

Chapter 11
Niani

I parked in front of Cameron's place and rushed out so fast, I forget to put the car in park. As soon as I put one foot on the ground, it started to roll backwards – with me halfway inside.

"Shit!"

I stepped on the brake and quickly shifted into park.

My heart was racing by the time I got to the front door. As soon as I started knocking, I realized the door wasn't completely closed.   I pushed it open and peeked inside.

"Cameron?"

Cautiously, I stepped in. I was worried that something bad had happened to him. He was a cop – and a paranoid one at that. It wasn't like him to leave his door open. I guess, given his mental state, it would be understandable. But as a precaution, I left his door partially open in case I needed to leave in a hurry.

The house looked as if a riot had passed through the neighborhood and left its mark in Cameron's living room.   Furniture was turned over.   Pictures ripped from the wall.   The lamp, which was still on, was on the floor, lighting the room at an awkward angle. Everything was out of order. The one picture left hanging on the wall was askew. His beloved "Nana," (dead for some 10 years now, I think) smiled at me. The toppled lamp—lighting half of her face while creating a shadow on the other side—caused her normally kind eyes to appear menacing. They seemed to be open just a little too much. Her smile was off in the light. A little too wide. The deranged robotic smile of a serial killer. The effect was disturbing.

Fear caused my mind to play tricks on me. I wondered to myself how many times Cameron had come across a scene like this. Was he as scared as I was? He couldn't have been because I was too scared to advance up the stairs. My heart pounded in my ears. My legs wouldn't move. Too afraid of what I would see.

"Cameron?" I called up the steps.

"Nia?" He responded weakly.

Concern trumped fear as I rushed up the stairs. The stairway was dark, but his room was lit. It took a second for my eyes to adjust to the light once I entered the room. I didn't see him at first, but then my eyes focused on the figure on the floor.

He was sitting in the corner behind the bed. His knees were pulled up to his face like a child – a child trying to escape a bad dream. His arms were wrapped around his knees. He looked impossibly small.

"Cameron?"

He lifted his head up. His eyes were blank and red. He smelled of alcohol.

"You came?" His voice was hoarse. It cracked as he spoke.

I went over to the floor and put my arms

around him.   Once there, I couldn't help but plant kisses all over his face.   There were no thoughts to my actions.   I was reacting out of pure love.   My heart was aching for him.   To see him in this position hurt more than I could ever imagine.   Nothing that happened between us in the past few weeks mattered.

"I didn't think you'd come.   I...I was scared to call you, but I needed you so much..."

"Shhhh, I'm here now, baby."

He wrapped his huge arms around my waist and leaned his head against my stomach. His hold on me tightened as he began to inhale and exhale hard.   Alcohol fumes escaped from his heavy breathing.   His nostrils flared with each breath.   His shoulders heaved up and down and his grip was uncomfortable – bordering on painful.   I started to get nervous as his respirations kept coming faster and faster.   Just as I thought he was going to pass out from hyperventilating, with his face still buried in my abdomen, he made a wailing sound.

"Baby, he's gone!   He's gone!   He's gone! He's gone!   I wasn't there to help him!"

Then he did something so unlike him that it scared the shit out of me.   He let down all of his guards and he cried.

"Adulterer."
Jaz

Chapter 12
Jasmine

Once, in this chat forum about cheating boyfriends, I saw that someone posted that married men were easier. You knew what to expect from them from the beginning, so you were never disappointed. Married men gave you all of the sex, the affection, and the gifts, with none of the drama.

It was probably a married man who left that post.

Adulterer.

That has been my secret title for most of my adult life. A person who commits adultery. No matter how many lives I impact through teaching, that will always cast a stain on my conscious. The scarlet letter "A" has not been branded on my clothes, but on my soul.

On my way home, I was so anxious, I was shaking. Everything I wanted to say to Curt – everything I kept contained in my heart – I was going to say tonight. I couldn't get home fast enough. I had waited far too long already.

So many lies!

I thought about all of the pain he caused

me over the years: from the minute, barely noticeable disappointments, to the heart-crushing revelations.

So much hurt.

I'd consumed so much of it that it saturated every cell in my body. Even the tips of my hair were swollen with pain. Pain was a part of my soul. It had shaped me. Changed me. Turned me into the insecure, self-doubting, meek, yes-woman that I am now.

I had no voice in the world, except in the classroom. There, whatever I said had meaning. I mattered. I made a difference. My decisions served a higher purpose. Everywhere else, my decisions couldn't be trusted; all because I chose to be with someone like Curtis.

The phone vibrated somewhere within the disaster zone that was my Murano. My poor truck was overrun with papers, opened mail, and empty water bottles. The leather passenger seat wasn't even visible. Money well spent. Apparently, I needed to clean up my life and my car.

"Shit!"

I had to swerve back into the lane before I ran into oncoming traffic. My phone was a lost cause.

I thought back to when I discovered that the family he claimed he dreamed of having with me was a reality he had with someone else. After that incident, he couldn't face me. He didn't even try. For seven months, the coward wouldn't so much as send an email.

My pride kept me from calling. The fact that he wasn't begging for my forgiveness and breaking down doors to talk to me added to my stubbornness.

The only things that helped were the kids

at school. Once I started teaching that fall, I threw myself into my students and my work. The kids looked up to me for guidance and answers. I was in control. I made up the rules. I was slowly reclaiming myself.

I should have left well enough alone.

Almost a year after that day in Dave and Busters, I was finally moving on with my life. I enjoyed my job, I had my own place, and I was no longer depressed over Curtis. In fact, I didn't think of him at all. My single life in full bloom, I no longer cried myself to sleep thinking about Curtis and his deception. There were two men that I was dating and one of them, Andre, I considered serious.

Right before Christmas, I got a text on my phone wishing me a Safe and Blessed Christmas. Even though I had long erased his number from my cell contacts, I still recognized it – and I felt nothing. I didn't bother to send a reply. Not out of anger; I just didn't see the point.

Three months after that text, He called. I didn't answer because my phone was in my purse and I was busy being stroked into orgasmic oblivion by my main boyfriend. I didn't notice the call until well after we were done.

"Damn, girl! I swear your pussy is so good, you're gonna have me incoherent and speaking in tongues one day."

"If so, it's probably because your old ass had a stroke," I teased.

Andre was 37 years old and I loved to tease him about his age. Not that I thought he was old, but because he was sensitive about the age difference - though he looked nowhere near 37. When we met, I thought he was about ten years younger. A former semi-pro football player, turned real estate investor, his body was tight as hell. And his love-making skills were off the chain!

"Whatever, Jaz." He laughed and rubbed my back as we talked. "This old-ass dick has you climbing the walls, huh?"

"Ummm, that it does! You know I'm just teasing, baby. You're not old."

"I know, but you're going to make me old if you keep draining me like this."

"No one told you to mess with this youngin'. If you can't handle it, maybe you should go find Eartha Kitt or somebody."

"I think I will, matter-of-fact."

I punched him in the chest and he laughed at me.

"Naw, for real. I heard Eartha's a freak!"

I pinched his ass hard.

"Ow! Why are you so violent? You lucky I can take pain."

"You're lucky I can, too, or you wouldn't be getting that anaconda anywhere near me."

"Umph! And you take it like a pro. You sure you haven't done porno's before? I knew your face looked familiar when we...Ouch! All right, baby, chill! I'm done. I forgot how violent the Red Man could be. Let me stop before you scalp my old ass."

"You better!"

"I think your phone was ringing a minute ago."

I got up and grabbed my purse while Dre was admired my naked form.

"Hmmm, I don't recognize the number," I said, even though I did.

"Maybe you should call it back. It could be

important."

"If it was that important, they would have left a message. Besides, I'm trying to get round two up and going." I crawled slowly on the bed towards him.

"That can definitely be arranged," Dre said as he grabbed my hips and positioned me on top of him.

Later that night, I got another call from Curt. I'm not sure why I answered, but I did. Curtis was on the other end, but he sounded different.   All of his cockiness gone, he sounded small and fragile.

"Why are you calling me?" I spoke to him in an angry whisper, trying not to wake Andre.

"I know I'm the last person you want to hear from, but please don't hang up. I need to talk to someone right now."

"What is it? Why do you want to talk to me? I'm kind of busy right now."

"My wife left me. She told me she was tired of being married and she just decided to leave."

"Well, I guess, I'm sorry to hear that, but what am I supp-..."

"Jasmine, she took my kids. I don't know where she's staying...I know our marriage is over...part of me is kind of relieved, but how could she just take my kids from me like that? I need them more than anything in this world! I feel like I'm going crazy without them!"

"Okay, but what do you want from..."

"Please, meet me, Jasmine! I just need to talk to someone face to face. Please...I know I don't deserve it, but do me this one favor. After that, if you want, I'll stay out of your life for good. I just need to see you."

I should have politely turned him down, but he stirred a strong emotion within me – pity. Feeling sympathy for him stirred up unresolved feelings that I thought had died with the previous year. I knew he was married, but I wasn't thinking about that - about his family. I only wanted to get rid of those damn feelings. So, I made one of the biggest mistakes of my life:

I agreed to meet him the next morning. What happened after that was...

The knock on my window startled me. I thought it was another random crackhead begging for gas money with no car.

"I'm sorry, but do you need some help? You've been sitting in your car for a minute and the pump has stopped."

"No, I was just daydreaming, I'll be out of your way in a ...." I stopped because recognized the guy outside of my door.

"Justin?"

It was the student teacher from Anne Kay's math class. The one all the girls had a crush on.

"Hey, Jasmine! I saw you when you got out to pump gas. You didn't move, so I wanted to make sure you were okay. What are you doing? About to go out?"

"Actually, I'm headed home. I have to take care of something."

"What? Go home? It's early! I know you're not tired."

"No, I'm not tired, I just..."

"Good, then you can follow me. I'm about to head out to The Lounge. I'm meeting some of my friends for my birthday."

"No, I really need to...oh, it's your birthday? Ummm, well, happy birthday. How old are you anyway?"

"The big 2-5! I'm getting old!"

"Yeah, a quarter of a century old!"

"You don't have to put it like that, damn!"

I laughed. "I'm sorry, but you need to enjoy yourself now. It's all downhill from now on. Take it from the wisdom of a 29 year-old ."

"Well in that case, I would enjoy myself even more if you joined me."

He smiled at me and I smiled back. I never realized how cute Justin was. No wonder the girls lost their minds around him. I thought it might not be that bad if hung out with him. Just then, I remembered that I was on my way to curse Curtis out and evict him permanently from my life.

"I'm sorry, Hon. I really should go home."

"Come on, Jaz! Don't make me beg! Not a good look. It's my birthday, you know." He imitated a sad child and poked his bottom lip out. Then he smiled, and I noticed how sexy of smile he had. With those dimples and perfect teeth, I lost my train of thought.

"So what do you say?"

I thought about and decided that Curt could wait. Tonight was the start of me being about me for a change.

"Where are we going again?"

"The Lounge. Follow me. Once my boy comes out of the store, we can leave."

A flash of white teeth and a pair of deep-set dimples had me mesmerized. I watched him walk back to his Maxima, caught in a trance.

"I might not even come home tonight," I thought to myself.

The vibrations from my phone brought me

out of my sinful thoughts. I frantically tossed papers out of the way and found it on the passenger side floor. I made a mistake and answered without looking. It was Curtis.

"Hey, baby!"

"Oh. Hello." I sounded as cold as I could, despite the slight palpitation in my heart when I heard his voice.

"Look, I know you're out with your girls and all, but I really need to see you now. Please come home, so I can..."

"Sorry, but we're about to go to another spot," I lied, "so I'll call you later."

"Wait! Please. I've been thinking about you all night. All week as a matter of fact."

"Hang up now!" A small voice inside my head tried to warn me, but curiosity got the better of me.

"And?" The sarcasm in my voice was strong, but he didn't seem fazed.

"I thought about everything that has happened with us and everything I've done to you. Jaz, I know I haven't been the best man. Actually, I've been downright shitty!"

"You got that right!"

"Baby, please, let me finish. I've been a piece of shit to you, but I want to make it better. I want to be the man that you need. Baby, please let me be that for you."

My façade began to crack. These were the words I've always dreamed of hearing him say to me. I fantasized about him finally realizing my worth.

"Where is all this coming from?" That little voice attempted to raise my suspicions, but the pull of my heart was too strong to resist.

"But...you've...you don't know how you've

hurt me so much all these years. I..."

"Baby, I know all this, and I want to make it up to you. Please give me this chance. Jaz, I'm filing for divorce this Monday!"

I tried to resist, but my spirit was so weak.

I was slipping.

"Really?" I said, hopefully.

I was falling.

"Really!" He confirmed.

I was lost.

That was it. I couldn't hold back any longer. This is what I wanted for so many years. It was really going to happen.

"I'm...I'm coming home."

Justin was still in his car waiting for his friend. I thought about leaving Curt waiting up for me. The way he's done me so many times.

I thought about it for only two seconds.

I walked over to Justin, and made up an excuse about feeling ill.

"Are you sure? Shoot, I really wanted to hang out with you."

"I know, but maybe another time."

"Do you need me to follow you home?"

I raised my eyebrows in suspicion.

"Not to get in your bed or anything. We can follow you before we go to spot. Just to make sure you get home safe."

"Thanks, but I'll be fine." I turned around to walk away before I had to create another lie.

"Wait! At least take my number. Text me when you get home and let me know that you're safe."

Wanting to decline, but not wanting to seem rude, I entered his number in my phone.

"Bye, have fun!"

"Roger that!"

I left as fast as I could. My new life with Curtis was starting, and I wasn't going to waste a minute of it without him.

This is what I'd hoped for. This is what I'd prayed for.

He wants me and only me.

I finally won.

"Then, why do I feel like such a loser?"

"I never lied about my situation."
Nia

Chapter 13:
Niani

I let him lay his head in my lap and cry.

He cried until my skirt was soaked and his eyes were dry.

I wanted badly to know exactly what happened, but I couldn't bring myself to ask. After what seemed like an eternity, he went over the details of his best friend's death.

To help his mom move, Cameron had switched shifts with his coworker, Andrew. Near the end of their normal shift, Kevin was patrolling with Andrew when they responded to a domestic disturbance call. On previous nights, Cameron and Kevin had responded to the Rawlings residence only to have Linda Rawlings answer the door with some sort of "self-inflicted" injury and Tony Rawlings nowhere to be found. She always blamed it on a fall, or a seizure, or even refused to speak. She never acknowledges she had been beaten.

This night, Kevin and his new partner arrived at the house, but no one answered the door. Kevin looked in the window to see Linda lying on the kitchen floor in a pool of blood and the foot of a man lying nearby. What he couldn't see was the Rawlings' 14 year-old son standing near the front door.   Andrew entered through the open back door and entered the kitchen to find Tony, Jr. standing over the body of his father, shaking and crying.   The officer was gently coaxing the skinny, frightened boy to drop the gun in his hand when Kevin suddenly kicked the front door open.   Hearing the loud noise, the boy swung around and the gun discharged – hitting Kevin in the stomach.   The bullet tore through his aorta and Kevin bled to death before help could arrive.

From the report he read, Tony, Sr., who had routinely beat his wife, had beaten her so severely that his son tried to intervene. After throwing his son into the wall and out of the way, a drunken Tony, Sr. continued to stomp his wife into a coma.   The son did the only thing he thought he could and grabbed his father's gun from under the mattress.   He ran back to the kitchen and pointed it at his dad, threatening to shoot if he didn't stop.   The father, thinking his son was bluffing, turned around to continue the abuse and was stopped by a bullet to the base of his skull.   The kid's junkie uncle was home and saw the whole thing.

The story was so sickening that I started to feel light-headed.   I couldn't even begin to fully grasp the fact that Kevin was dead.

"I got to Shock/Trauma just in time to see them cover my man with a sheet.   I couldn't believe that they had given up already, and I started yelling at them to take the sheet off - you know - and do their damn jobs.   One of my boys pulled the sheet back so I could see.   When I saw his face and how blank his eyes were, Drew had to grab me to keep me from falling.   Everyone was crying and sobbing, but I was shaking! I was so angry, Nia! Everyone was comforting each other, but I wanted to hurt somebody. I wanted to hurt the little punk responsible."

I wasn't so sure that I wanted him to continue, but I was too scared to speak. Bracing myself to hear what was next, I let him continue.

"I left my colleagues at the hospital and drove back to the precinct with one thought in my head. I needed to see this boy. I needed to put my hands on him and cause him some of the pain he's caused so many people. Once I found out which holding room he was in, nothing could stop me. I ran back to that room and opened the door so hard, it slammed into the wall. He stood up instantly and stared at me with eyes wide with fear. And then, I really saw him. In my mind, he was this thug-ass little punk who was no stranger to crime; who deserved to get his ass kicked. Instead, what I saw was this young, skinny kid with glasses – a kid who lived his life in fear - handcuffed to the table. I tried to look past all that and just stay mad. I wanted to hurt this kid so badly.

I balled up my fists and stepped towards him. Then, I looked at his disheveled clothes and noticed a dried dark stain at his crotch. It was old piss. He pissed his pants probably when he shot his own father. I...I couldn't take another step in that room. He was just as much a victim as Kevin, or his mother. One low-life, worthless, woman-beating son-of-a-bitch caused all of this pain – not him! That boy didn't deserve to be hurt anymore by anybody.

Nia, I couldn't take it. I s-started crying. Right there in front of him, I started bawling like a baby. All of the commotion brought other officers in the room and I had to get the hell out of there! I came home and got a drunk as I could. Took my rage out on my house. When I was done, I couldn't think of what else to do, so I called you. I'm sorry. I didn't mean..."

"Shhhh." I lifted his head up and kissed him. I didn't know of anything else I could do to help. I couldn't take him being in so much pain.

He returned my kiss hard and roughly pushed back until I was lying on the floor. His kisses were different. Not his usual smooth and seductive style, they were desperate. It was as if he needed me so bad, he was trying to inhale me. His hands moved frantically over my body, almost ripping my clothes off. He kissed me and cried at the same time. My face was wet with tears and saliva.

This wasn't the Cameron I knew. His shield broken, he was exposed. He wasn't about appearances right now. He was a body of pure need. Unashamed in his clumsiness. His intense passion scoring me with every rough kiss and forceful touch.

My body was on fire with this unexpected assault of raw fervor. My need to be with him was as strong as his need to be with me. I couldn't get his clothes off quick enough. His helplessness stirred something primal within me and I wanted to protect him in the worst way. I wanted to shelter him from his pain as much as I could, for as long as I could.

I pushed him onto his back. Undoing his pants, I started licking the line of hair from his navel on down. The huge bulge that his erection created made my mouth water. I couldn't waste my time by teasing him. I had to taste him. I snatched his pants down and greedily took him in my mouth. I devoted my attention to the head, sucking the precum that was already seeping out.

"Ohhhhhh! God!"

Something took over me. His moans and words of praise coinciding with his tears excited me beyond measure. I licked the sensitive spot under the head.

"Yesssss," he hissed.

I worked my tongue over his shaft as I slid it in and out. I took in as much as I could – fighting like hell against my gag reflex. The ridges of its distended veins pulsing inside my mouth. I could feel him tensing and I was torn. I wanted to taste him so bad, but I needed to feel this hardness deep inside of me. As much as I wanted to give him release, I took the selfish route and pulled up.

"Wha...Baby, what are you doing. I was about to cum."

"Shhhh. It's okay, baby," I gently cooed in his ear. He was under *my* control tonight and I was not letting it go to waste.

I straddled him and started grinding back and forth on his swollen member. The heat and slickness of my aching slit threatened to make me lose it right there. I put one leg up to position his entry and took in his 12 inches, inch by painfully sweet inch. I allowed his thick penis to stretch my walls to capacity.

Cameron moaned and grabbed my hips to push me down, but I resisted. Unable to maintain control, he lifted his pelvis and hastened his entry.

I bit my lip against the pain and dug my nails into his ribs. Using his chest as leverage, I started riding him slow – taking my time to bring him to orgasm. He closed his eyes (tears falling

as he did) and arched his back against my stroking.   He grabbed my hips and held them so
tightly, I had to stifle a cry of pain.   I was wet
beyond belief, the secretions running down my
legs and the sides of his abdomen.

He slid both hands up my back and
grabbed my shoulders.   He pulled me down
enough to lift my shirt up and take an erect nipple into his warm mouth.   Gently sucking, he
moved his tongue in a wave-like motion over the
sensitive flesh.   In between moans, he alternated
to the other breast, leaving the abandoned one to
tingle in the cool air.

I couldn't take it. I got up on both feet and
started riding him fast and hard.   I was ready.
He was ready.

We both needed this.

I moved up and down hard.   My ass
bounced on his thighs and made a soft slapping
sound.   I reached back and grabbed his heavy
scrotum, wet from my secretions, gently kneading
it with my fingers.   The combined sensations were
too much for him.   His stomach and balls tightened.   I knew he was about to cum, but it didn't
matter. I was already there.

At the last second, he thrust himself all the
way inside me, and we both came in unison.
Each spasmodic thrust of his organ caused an
orgasmic spasm of mine.   Paralyzed, I couldn't
move. My body locked in the throes of a climactic
seizure.   The pleasure seemed to carry on for minutes without wavering, and then, it was gone.

I collapsed on top of him, gasping for air.
He held my head to his chest and softly kissed
my forehead.   The raw, unabashed passion of the
entire act was so intense.   So beautiful.   I experienced a connection deeper than I ever had be-

fore.

He lifted my head up and looked in my eyes. An amazed, confused look was over his face. I could tell he was feeling the same way. He slid me up his body so I could reach his face, and took me with his full, soft lips. His kisses were passionate, but gentle. We carefully tasted each other's tongues, and I felt the most peace I have ever felt since childhood.

The feelings were overwhelming. This was him. The man that I wanted. Needed. Loved with every being of my soul. I couldn't deny it any longer. We were meant to be.

"I love you so much, Niani! I've never felt this for any other woman. I need you in my life – full time. Please give me a chance. Don't leave me again. We can do this, baby."

I kissed him to cut him off – hoping to stop him before his words had me considering something crazy. But it was too late.

"I'm too far gone to turn back. Maybe we can make this work. Oh Lord, what am I going to tell James? What about..."

"Oh my God! Oh my God! What are you doing?"

A high-pitched, shrill voice interrupted my thoughts and scared the shit out of me. Caught off guard, I turned around to see a tall, thick woman standing in the doorway with a horrified look.

"Cameron! What the fuck is going on?" Tears started to form in her eyes. The shocked woman looked at Cameron, then me, then back to Cameron. She glanced at my skirt pulled up around my waist, his pants pulled down below his own, and our exposed genitals. She began to cry even harder.

My mind tried to process the situation as quickly as possible. I stared at the woman and took in as much as I could. Honey-brown skin. Long brown hair. Narrow mouth. Wide nose. Light brown eyes. Bushy eyebrows. Thick, but with a nice hourglass shape. Very tall. Maybe they were related.

I turned to Cameron to ask him who the hell she was, but he spoke first.

"What are you doing here?" His words came out harsh. He didn't look happy.

"What do you mean? Why are you asking me that? Who the fuck is this, Cameron?"

"What are you doing here?" he said louder. I got up, confused. I tried to pull my skirt down to cover my ass, but for some reason, it wouldn't move beyond mid-way. Cameron stood up, grabbed the sheet off the bed to cover me, and pulled his stained pants up. He never took his eyes off the woman.

"What the fuck are you doing here?"

He said it with so much anger that the woman and I both jumped. The tables had turned. Suddenly, she was on the defensive.

"I-I-I heard what happed to Kevin. I...I...couldn't get in touch with you. You didn't answer your phone, and I was worried, boo."

"Boo?"

"When I got here, the door was open, and...and I was scared something happened or you did something to yourself?"

I remembered I forgot to close the front door. I left it open in case I needed a quick escape.

"You know better than to just show up at my place."

He took a couple of steps closer to her and

she backed up towards the hallway. He was so angry right now I thought he might hit her.

"I was worried! What did you think I would do?" As if mentally reliving the scene she just walked into, her voice held a little more courage. She stood her ground. "I see why you didn't..."

Still confused, I interrupted her accusation. "Wait, wait, wait one fucking minute! Who is this, Cameron?"

Things were starting to become clearer, and I was beginning to see red.

Cameron turned to face me and grabbed my hands – either to prepare me, side with me, or keep me from slapping him.

"I'm his girlfriend," the tall bitch said with a smirk, before he could speak.

"Ex-girlfriend!" Cameron responded. He turned to face her and said, "And that's using the term loosely."

Her expression turned back to hurt. "Who the fuck is *she*, Cameron?" She spoke in a high-pitched, irritating voice that cut through my ears and made my head ache.

He ignored her question and turned back to me, still holding my hand. "Baby, this is an ex. We still messed with each other once in awhile, but nothing more. She and I..."

"I thought you told me you didn't have a girlfriend?" I asked him, searching his eyes for the truth.

"I told you, she's my ex. I don't have a girlfriend. It was sex and nothing more. I wanted you. Always wanted you from the moment I saw you in the mall."

"Nothing more?" She was on the verge of tears again. "So all the time we spent together...? I bought you things. Cleaned for you. Cooked for you. All the times we made love?"

"Fucked! We fucked! It was sex! You knew that!" He turned back to me.

"So you were fucking somebody else?" I couldn't believe what was going on.

"You're engaged!" The absurdity of it all hit him and he raised his hands in exasperation. "What was I supposed to do? I wanted more, but you didn't. I could only see you on certain days, call you at certain times..."

"I was honest with you from the beginning! I never lied about my situation! You could've given me the same consideration!"

"I know, Babe, and I'm sorry. I should have been honest. I just didn't think you cared about what I did when we weren't together."

"What about when *we* were together? What about everything you said to me?" Feeling left out of the loop, the woman interrupted our heart-to-heart. "I thought you wanted to be with me."

"I never said that!" He turned his back on her once more. "Look, Nia, there are things about me that you don't know, but I want to be honest. Let's go somewhere and talk. I want you to give us a chance and we can..."

"But what about the baby?"

"Baby?"

We both looked at her.

"Shut the fuck up, Alicia!"

Knowing exactly what she was doing, she kept going.

"Are you just going to leave us for this ho who's sleeping with two men?"

Too stunned to acknowledge her insult, I turned to Cameron with confusion in my eyes and pain in my heart.

"Baby?" I could barely choke out the words. I blinked hard trying to stave off the tears.

Cameron stared at me. His mouth opened and closed, but nothing came out. Like he didn't know where to begin.

"I'm pregnant. Four months pregnant with his child."

Neither of us looked at her this time. I knew she was trying to bring attention back to her.

Cameron closed his eyes and took a deep breath before he spoke.

"Yes, she's pregnant."

I blinked back tears of disbelief. "What? But why didn't you...How did...Oh my God, Cameron, pregnant?"

"I didn't know how to tell you. At first, we talked about it and she said she was getting an abortion. Then she changed her mind, and I...I didn't know what to do. Baby, I told you we're not together. It was just sex, but I wasn't careful."

I pulled my hand away and backed away from him in horror, shaking my head. "Pregnant? How could you do this to me? How could you not tell me? Y-You...you never loved me did you?"

"Baby, please don't say that. I love you so much. I was scared. I didn't know what to do. I was just trying to win you over, and I knew if you found out, there was no way..."

"You're damn right there was no fucking way I would be with you! You're a fucking liar! And a dog! And you played the shit out of me! I can't believe I fell for you! I can't believe I trusted you!"

"But, you had someone. You..."

"So that gave you the right to lie to me?"

"No, that's not what I meant."

"I can't believe this! I can't fucking believe this!"

I couldn't control my emotions anymore. The tears came so hard, I could barely see. I searched to room for my things and grabbed them in a hurry.

"Don't go, Nia! Please, we have to talk about this."

"Why are you asking her not to go? What about me, Cameron? What about all the things you said to me?" That high-pitched voice was making me nauseous.

"Not now, Alicia! You and me are done! There's nothing between us, but this child. You knew that...Wait, Nia. Don't leave yet!"

I couldn't listen to anymore of this. All of a sudden, I felt flushed. Lightheaded. The room started spinning. My stomach was turning. I had to get out of that house.

I felt like the world's biggest fool.

I rushed out of his room, pushing past the big pregnant chick who shattered my dreams of spending my life with Cameron. Before I could get in my car, Cameron came out of nowhere and grabbed my arm.

"Baby, please! I'm begging you not to leave. We can talk about this. I need you. Only you. Give me a chance. I promise, I'll..."

"You'll what? What can you possibly do to make this right? Nothing, Cameron, so don't even try. You wanna do something right? Then, leave me the fuck alone!"

And with that, I snatched my arm back, jumped in my Solara, and drove out of Baltimore as fast as I could.

Speeding away from this soul-crushing re-
velation and out of Cameron's life for good.

> "...my mind had me thinking that everyone
> there knew..."
>
> Taz

Chapter 14:
Tazanna

I followed her to the Marriott parking lot
with all of my conflicted feelings in tow – guilt,
excitement, shame, anticipation, arousal.   I
couldn't believe I was doing this again.

She's too intoxicating.

Too addicting.

I decided in my mind that this was going to
be the last time. Now, I just needed to convince
the rest of my body.

She walked over to my truck, and I rolled
my window down. She bent in the window to
speak to me, and cleavage almost spilled out of
her dress. A single blonde-tipped lock fell into
the crevice between. Without thought, I licked
my lips, wishing it was my tongue there instead.

"Wait here while I get us a room."

I kept my mind busy while she was gone,
so I wouldn't start feeling guilty again. I was
thinking about my schedule for Monday, when
she knocked back on my window.

"Let's go, Sexy!"

I walked through the lobby with her, nervously scanning the area for someone who could recognize me. I saw no one I knew.

Still, my mind had me thinking that everyone there knew we were fucking.

I thought, *"What if people think we're lesbians?"*

Suddenly, I was more afraid of being recognized as a lesbian than an adulterer. I wasn't ready to be open to public opinion. Just because I'm attracted to women doesn't mean I'm gay.

I still love men.

"This is stupid. You came here to have a good time and now you're battling with your sexual identity? It's just fun – nothing more."

We stepped on the elevator with a portly older white man. As soon as the doors shut, Corrine started lightly caressing the back of my neck with her fingers. I closed my eyes and let the sensation move down my body and create goose bumps in its trail.

She leaned towards me and kissed the nape of my neck.

The man behind us shifted. Cleared his throat. I could hear his breathing speed up a little, and I knew he was watching.

Corrine did, too, because she got bolder and slipped her hand in my top. Her fingers felt their way to my nipple, and they began to gently roll it back and forth. I couldn't help myself and let out a soft moan. I could hear the man in back moving, and I wondered what he thought of the whole situation. The thought of him witnessing our intimacy heightened my excitement.

The doors to the elevator opened on a floor that was not ours. Corrine pulled her hand back and we composed ourselves. No one entered the elevator, so we looked back at the man. He was red-faced. Tiny beads of perspiration formed on his forehead and cheeks. When he realized it was his floor, he let out an embarrassed, "Oh," gave us an awkward smile and quickly exited.

We both giggled as the doors closed.

"He's probably going to jerk off as soon as he gets in his room."

I agreed. Or maybe he was going to wake up some poor, sleeping old woman.

"Maybe she would get the best 2 minutes of her elderly life," I thought.

We stepped off the elevator onto our floor. The exhibitionist display of affection turned me on more than I could ever have imagined. The only thing on my mind was getting her inside and burying my face between her warm, brown thighs.

As soon as we were in the room, we both started undressing. I unbuttoned my pants, and she helped by pushing them to my ankles while licking from my navel, down my warm flesh, and stopping at the slit – just millimeters above my throbbing clit.

I sighed in frustration, which made her chuckle at my impatience.

"I think you owe me something," she said playfully.

Corrine stood up and pulled her dress above her waist. Her body was so perfect, I felt a pang of jealously the first time I saw her naked. We both wear a size 36DD, but she is blessed with the tiniest waist, and an ass so round, it brings men to their knees.

She took off her thong and pulled me onto the bed. Legs spread apart, she laid there inviting me. Taunting me. I slid my body on top of hers and reveled in its softness. Her sweet aroma made me high. She smelled like lavender and honey. I wanted to taste every inch of her, but couldn't wait. My mouth went straight to the heat between her thighs. I opened the lips and pulled the flesh back – exposing the sensitive bud underneath. I started gently flicking the flesh with my tongue and she began to squirm beneath me. Getting lost in the moment, I pulled her clitoris into my mouth and started gently sucking, while still flicking it with my tongue.

"Ohhhhh! Mmmm!"

Her moans were turning me on. She gently intertwined her fingers in my hair and pulled me in closer. My hands slid outward to her thighs and spread them wider. Lifted them higher. I wanted to make her cum hard, so I started to pick up the pace.

My clit ached bad; I needed release. I reached one of my hands between my legs and began rubbing it. I took my middle finger and inserted as far inside me as I could go. It was so hot. Wet. I wished Terrence was there with us in the room. I pictured him holding my hips, spreading my cheeks apart, and entering me slowly. I pictured him stroking me deeply as I burrowed my tongue inside Corrine. Bringing her to her climax while Terrence brought me to mine.

So caught up in the moment, I barely heard the knock at the door. I picked my head up, which made Corrine cry out in frustration.

"No, don't stop! God, I was almost about to..."

The person knocked again, but this time it was louder – more intense. It startled us both, and I jumped to my feet. I pulled my jeans up, and went to the door and looked out the peep hole.

"I don't see anybody."

Corrine chuckled. "It was probably some silly kid playing a prank. Come back to bed."

I agreed, but cracked the door open to be sure. I peeped down the hall to see if I could catch any kids running for the stairwell. Without warning, a figure came into my view and pushed himself in the room. He caught me off guard and I lost my balance. I fell back, and hit my elbow on the wall.

"Owww!"

Unsuccessfully, I reached out for something to stop my fall, but instead, clumsily landed on my butt.

All of the commotion caught Corrine's attention, and she got up.

"What the fuck is..." Before she could finish her sentence, the words were caught in her throat by the sight of the wild-eyed, disheveled man before her.

Even though I knew what was happening, I didn't want to believe it.

"Jason? What the fuck...?

"What the fuck am *I* doing here?" Hmmph! What the fuck am *I* doing here? Is that what you were going to ask me?" He laughed, but there was no humor in it. "Funny! That's what I was about to ask you!"

Somehow, Corrine's husband followed us here. I stood up slowly, rubbing my elbow. I was too scared to breathe for fear of bringing any attention to myself. I was terrified, but couldn't move. Not knowing his mental state, I didn't want to leave Corrine alone with him.

His normally impeccable wavy hair was disheveled and stringy. Stray pieces clung to the sweat on his face. He looked as if he hadn't shaved in days and his piercing green eyes were dull and glassy. The smell of alcohol was strong, and I didn't need a breathalyzer to know that he was drunk.

He looked at the state of Corrine's dress as she nervously pulled it down to cover her nakedness.

"Sweetie, I...I...thought y-you were out of..."

"Out of town? Yup, that's what I told you. That's what I wanted you to think."

He looked at me, then back at Corrine.

"I knew something was up, but I had to see it with my own eyes. I...knew you were cheating, but this...with her? Why?"

He brought his hands up and covered his face. He breathed heavy and began to sob. I wanted to feel some sympathy for this man – some guilt for what I did to his marriage – but I was too afraid for my own safety. Instead, I noticed the dirt under his nails and felt only a slight feeling of disgust. Ashamed at myself, I looked away from him and down at my bare feet.

Corrine went to him. Her eyes filling with salt water, she tried to explain herself.

"It's not your fault. I've felt this way about women for as long as I can remember. I never meant to hurt you or the kids. I never wanted to...I love you so much, I..."

She reached out and made the mistake of putting her hand on his shoulder. Her touch must have burned like fire, because instantly, he pulled away and a scowl crossed his face. I knew what was coming, but my legs turned to lead; I couldn't react in time. He backhanded her so fast, I didn't have time to blink.

Corrine flew back and flipped over the bed. He went after her and was on her before she could come to a complete stop.

"Don't touch me, you lying bitch! You're fucking lying! You never loved me, did you?"

His hands went to her neck and closed around it. Choking her. Finally, I could move. I started to scream.

"Let her go! You're killing her, let her go!"

I tried to pull him away, but he wouldn't budge. Then, he let her go, reached back, and grabbed my hair – used it to hold my head back, so I could look him in the eyes.

There was nothing in them.

"You lesbian bitch! I let you in my home! Let you watch my kids! You smiled in my face! All the while, you were fucking my wife!"

He pushed me back hard, and I stumbled into the chair. The sensation from my knee hitting the seat was so excruciating, I thought something had broke. The pain made my eyes water.

Satisfied with the results of his rage towards me, he returned his attention to his wife.

Corrine pulled herself to her feet, coughing and pulling for air. When she saw that Jason was now facing her, she backed up towards the wall, reached out to the side, and without looking, grabbed the lamp on the nightstand.

"Back the fuck up, motherfucker!"

Oblivious to the threat of an impending concussion, her husband took a step towards her.

"Wasn't I good enough for you? Good enough to you?"

This time, his voice was soft. It cracked with pain. He was pleading to deaf ears.

Corrine was not taking any chances as she

slowly raised the lamp above her head.

"I said...back...the fuck...up!"

Jason took another unsteady step towards her.

"I...love you so much. Was it because I was working too much? I shouldn't have left you and the girls alone for so long. Honey, I can do better. I'll quit the firm, and...and work for the state. I-If you want, we...I can do th-..."

Corrine wasn't waiting for his sensitive moment to pass. I watched in horror as the lamp swung full force, and the metal base collided with his the right side of his jaw and temple. I heard a pop, and Jason spun around 180 degrees and hit the floor. The light bulb flashed brighter, but miraculously, did not break.

Corrine was breathing heavy, looking over the body of her husband. She looked at me, still on the floor.

"Are you okay?"

I stood up, dazed. I looked over at Jason and saw blood trickling from his ear and mouth. A gash was on the side of his head. I couldn't see any movement in his chest, but I sure as hell wasn't going over there to check.

"I'm okay. I-I-..." The reality of everything hit me. My hands started shaking, and I thought I would start crying until...

More banging. Shuffling at the door. The electronic key lock beeped and the door opened.

"Are you guys okay in there? I called 911. The police are on their way."

A small man, about 5'5" carefully pushed the door open. He had on a suit and a hotel badge. Someone must have heard the commotion and called the front desk.

"We're okay. It was a...a domestic issue.

Thank you. Please call an ambulance, as well."

Corrine put her game face back on. There was no fear or hysteria in her voice. She was calm and collected, even if her appearance was frightening.

She wiped the blood off the side of her mouth and attempted to smooth her locks.

"My husband...he attacked us. I had to hit him to stop him from choking me." Her eyes blankly focused on the wall as she said this. The realization of what could have happened must have hit her. The moment lasted for a split second and then she looked at me.

"Are you okay?"

I followed her eyes to my elbow, which was already turning blue and purple. Looking at it made me aware of the throbbing pain that I hadn't noticed just moments before.

Broken blood vessels leaking blood beneath tissue. Damaged cells, leaking fluid and causing edema. Pain neurons signaling something is wrong. Fight or flight response wearing off. Endorphin production decreasing, taking the natural pain relief with it. The same process was happening with my injured knee.

My mind focused on science to block out any emotion.

"I'm okay."

But really, I wasn't.

She reached down to feel for a pulse. I held my breath – expecting her to tell me she couldn't feel one. Without warning, he shot to his feet as if nothing had happened. Corrine jumped back and went for the lamp again. Jason looked around the room, trying to gather his wits. He looked at me, the hotel manager, and then the crowd of people gathering outside of the door in the hallway. Suddenly, he bolted out of the room, knocking stunned bystanders into the wall as he went. He left the room as quickly as he entered.

"Hey! Stop! You can't leave. The police are on their way!" The hotel manager and two other male employees went chasing after him.

An older Indian woman came in the room to make sure we were all right, but the remaining guests stared into the room through the propped door. No one else dared to enter.

"Oh my goodness, Dear! Are you okay?" She went to the bruise on my arm that incredibly looked worse than it felt.

"I'm okay. Really, ma'am, you don't have to..." I was beginning to feel a little faint. I looked down at my feet for balance and noticed that my pants were still unbuttoned. I turned away from the crowd to adjust my clothes.

The people in the hall were talking as if Corrine and I weren't in the room.

"What happened?"

"I just heard this loud bang, and then a woman screamed..."

"Boom! Like someone kicked in the door..."

"That guy was the husband to one of the women and he..."

"...think they were having an affair, and he walked in..."

"...saw them when they came in. They definitely came together, and they were holding hands and..."

I felt like a spectacle. Everyone knew I just got my ass kick for having an affair with a married woman.

They knew we were lovers.

They knew I slept with a woman.

I had to get out of there.

I looked around the room and saw my purse and shoes. I grabbed them and ran out as fast as I could.

"Taz!"

I ran to the entrance to the stairwell, not wanting Corrine to catch me at the elevator. I had to get home.

"What time is it? What am I going to tell Terrence? How do I explain these bruises?"

All of these thoughts were going through my head as I passed the confused people in the hotel lobby. I had just made it to the parking lot when Corrine caught up to me and grabbed my arm.

"Wait! Taz, where are you going? You're not going to go home like that, are you? You have to go to the hospital to make sure you're okay. You fell pretty hard and you...You're still limping."

"I'm fucking okay! Okay? How many times do I have to say that? I just need to get the fuck out of here before your crazy-ass husband decides to come back for another shot at second degree murder!"

"Look, I know this was bad, but, baby, at least it's out in the open. We...we don't have to hide anymore. We can be together – stop pretending!"

"Pretending what? Be what? Be together? Are you as crazy as Jason? What the hell? Do you really...expect me to leave my husband? My family? For what? For you? For sex? 'Cause that's all we had. Nothing more! Nothing less!"

Corrine reeled back like I had slapped her. Her bottom lip trembled and tears started to form.

"Don't say that, Taz. I know you feel something. Maybe not as much I do, but I know. I love you. I've loved you every since college." She stepped towards me and placed her palms on the sides of my face. Made me look into her eyes as they searched mine for some sort of confirmation.

"Well I don't love you! At least not in the way you're..." I was interrupted by the voice of a man behind me.

"Taz?"

I turned around in the direction of the voice, expecting to be sucker-punched by Corrine's husband.

Instead, I saw my own husband staring at me in confusion and disbelief.

He was dressed in a suit. The dark blue one that I liked so much. He looked so handsome.

He had a bouquet of pink roses in his hand. My favorite kind.

"Terrence? What..."

"Jason told me to meet you up here. He said you had a surprise for me." Choking back emotion, he cleared his throat. "I-I-I thought...y-you were trying to be romantic. Had your mom come over to watch the girls..."

I could see it in his eyes. He saw Corrine and my little "love spat" in the parking lot. He knew.

"Oh, God, Terrence! Wait! Please don't...It's not what you think."

He looked at me, then Corrine, then back at me. He swallowed hard.

"So this is what you two do together?"

He let the roses fall from his hand onto the asphalt. Tears formed in his eyes, making the light from the street lamp twinkle in them.

"You don't understand. I...I'm so sorry!" I took a step towards him, vaguely aware that he could react just as violently as Jason, but not concerned. I stretched both my arms out to him. Palms up. A sign of submission. A plea for forgiveness.

"Please, let me explain..."

But I had no explanation for this.

He knew this, too.

Terrence stepped back, solemnly shaking his head. He took his glasses off and wiped his eyes. A look of unspeakable pain was in them. It was a look I had never seen from anyone - much less my husband.

Just that quick, it hit me.

My marriage was over.

I stopped walking and dropped my hands to my sides.

The pressure of everything – the night's events, the years of lying, the double life – bubbled up within and released itself through a torrent of tears. For the first time since I was a little girl, I cried.

Life, as I knew it, was over.

There was no going back.

My legs lost all strength and gave way from under me. I fell to my knees, sobbing uncontrollably and hugging myself for sanity.

Terrence took a few more steps backwards, never taking his eyes off me. Then slowly, he turned, bowed his head, and walked out of the harsh, artificial light.

Into the protective darkness of the steamy summer's night.

"If this was karma, then my debt was paid in full."
Nia

Chapter 15:
Niani

Once again, I was speeding down the BW Parkway, but this time I wasn't nervous. I was devastated. So angry and hurt, I was shaking. I couldn't believe what had just happened.

"A baby? Why didn't he tell me? How could I have not known he was seeing someone else? Why did I come back tonight? How could I be so stupid?"

My mind shot the same questions at me over and over.

I couldn't focus. Couldn't think.

My heart was aching so bad, I couldn't catch my breath. Tears blinded my vision. I wiped at them frantically, but it did no good. They came as quickly as I wiped. I pulled over onto the shoulder so I could compose myself before I hit another living creature.

I needed to talk to Taz. I couldn't see to work the phone, so I tried the Solara's Bluetooth.

"Call Taz."

"Pardon?" The computerized woman responded in confusion. My voice was hoarse from yelling and crying. Combined with the mucous in my throat, it made me unintelligible.

I cleared my throat. "Call Taz!"

"Dialing..."

The phone rang and rang as I prayed for her to pick up.

"Hello..."

"Taz! I nee-..."

"...you have reached Tazanna Kearnan, I'm sorry that I can't..."

"Shit! Shit! Shit! Fucking voicemail!" I hung up.

I needed to talk to someone, anyone. I thought about James, and suddenly needed to hear his voice. I didn't want to call him like this and try to explain why I was so upset, but I had to talk to him.

I thought about all of the lies. The deceptions. This was my punishment for cheating on a good man. I made up my mind that I was going to tell him the whole story and prayed that he would forgive me.

"Call James!"

"Dialing..."

"The number you have reached has been temporarily disconnected..."

"Shit!" I forgot he'd lost his phone. I searched my phone contacts for his brother's house phone. It was nowhere to be found. As usual, I entered the number and forgot to save it.

The only other useful number I had was the one to his 24-hour Laundromat. Hoping a sympathetic employee would answer and give me his info, I called.

"Hello?" A woman with a heavy Spanish accent answered the phone.

"Hello? Is this the Black Diamonds Laundromat? I need to speak with James!"

"Eh? Oh noooo. Meeser James no is

here."

"Yes, yes, I know he's not there, but I really need to speak to him! Can you please give me his phone number?"

"Oh, Meeser James no has phone. Is lost. Is home sleeping."

I wasn't getting anywhere. I thought back to my two years of high school Spanish and my on the job lessons from Maria.

"I know! Please, this is his fiancé…um, soy su novia!" I think that was the word for fiancé in Spanish.

"Si?"

"Por favor! Necessito…uh…el numero del telephono…, um… a su casa. Es una emergencia!"

"Emergencia? Si, si. Un momento!"

I waited for a few seconds until she returned to the phone.

"Seis, …"

"En Inglés, por favor." My Spanish was not good enough to be able to correctly translate a telephone number.

"Si, lo siento! Six…" She finished the rest of the numbers in English, and I thanked her profusely.

I dialed and waited for someone to answer. At this time of night, I knew I would probably wake James' brother and sister-in-law, but I didn't care.

"Hello?" A woman, still groggy from the spell of deep sleep, answered the phone.

"Hi, I'm so sorry to be calling so late, but this is Nia, and I really need to speak with James."

"Who? James?"

"I'm really sorry to wake you up, but could

you please put James on the phone? This is Nia-ni!"

"Who?"

"His fiancé! Don't you remember? We met..."

"Wait a minute, his what? You want to speak to James Wright?"

"Yes! This is his..."

"Fiance? I don't understand..."

"I'm sorry. I thought I was speaking to Kim, Jonathan's wife."

"Um, no. This is Lauren."

"Oh, I'm sorry. I must have..."

"James' girlfriend."

"James' what?" I thought that I heard wrong. I chuckled humorlessly into the phone.

"His girlfriend."

Then reality sunk in.

"Is this some type of joke? What the hell...? I'm his fiancé! We're engaged! We've been together for almost eight years!"

"We've been together for two and a half!"

My head was about to explode.

"He's been talking about moving up here with me to run his business fulltime and opening another laundromat. This is my house that you called."

I couldn't believe this was happening to me. The tears began to flow again.

"Where the fuck is James? What the hell is going on?"

"That's a very good question. You can ask him yourself since he just walked through the door. Telephone, James!"

I could hear his voice in the background. "What are you doing still up? Who's calling me? Is it someone from Diamonds?"

"It's Niani!"

There was silence and then, I heard him take the phone.

"Nia? Hey, b-babe, what...how did you get this number? "

"Baby?" I heard Lauren in the background, confused and angry.

"A girlfriend? So this is what you do when you go to Jersey?"

"Babe, I can explain. I..."

Lauren was yelling at him as he was trying to speak. "Babe? You need to be explaining to me! You're engaged! I can't believe this! I trusted you, you piece of shit! Gave you money to start Black Diamonds! Even thought about moving..."

He must have moved away from her because her words were coming from the distance now. The sound of a door slamming and then, someone banging on it.

"Nia, listen..."

"Listen to what? What can you say to me, James? What explanation could you possibly have for this?"

The feeling of numbness was setting in quickly and the tears finally began to dry.

"And here I thought you were distant because of your work. Here I was feeling guilty because I wanted more time with you! I never figured you had another life!"

"Baby, I don't have another life."

More banging in the background. Yelling.

I felt nothing

I opened and closed my hands, but my fingers were numb. I could feel movement, but no sensation.

"You are my life!"

I looked out into the night and saw only blackness ahead of me.

I felt nothing.

"This...she didn't mean anything to me."

No red tint. No blue glow. No hint of color. No synesthesia.

Nothing.

"Just someone to spend time with while I was away, missing you."

I felt nothing.

"I know, that...that was so selfish and ir-responsible of me, but I-I-I never planned to con-tinue it. I was just letting off steam before we got married. I..."

"It's over."

Where numbness began, clarity ended.

The missed calls. The money not adding up. All of those monthly trips out of town. The lavish gifts when he returned. It all started to make sense.

"Baby, no! Don't...we can..."

"I'm not marrying you."

"Okay, we don't have to get married now. We can start over! Go to counseling! Give me the chance to prove..."

"It's done. There no future for us, James. I'm done."

I wasn't angry. I wasn't hurt. No, forget that. I was hurt, but not enough to make me think twice about what I was doing. I just wanted out.

There was one too many people in this re-lationship, and it wasn't Lauren.

I was the one who didn't belong.

More banging in the background.

"No! Wait...please!" He lowered his tone. His voice was wavering. Shaky. It broke as if he was holding back a sob. "I'm on my way home right now."

"I loved you, James Wright."
And with that, I ended the call.
Turned my phone off.
Kept driving.

If this was karma, then my debt was paid in full.

Serenity Interrupted

The light of day dims overhead;
Above, lie hues of orange
And red; Below,
The view of
Setting
Sun,
Another day without you, gone.

Addie

Chapter 16:
Niani

Standing in front of my car, I started to get that feeling again: the "walking a tightrope above the ocean" butterflies. Except, this time, there was no excitement - only nervousness. And sadness. This meeting was the beginning of closure.

I knew I was going to fall. It felt like I was falling already.

Waiting there to meet Cameron, I was getting more restless by the minute. I agreed to meet him in person one last time and already, I was regretting it.

The last four months without any contact from him had allowed me to think with a clear head. The first month was the hardest, but it got easier with each week. There was a time when he ruled my thoughts so much, it was an accomplishment every time I realized that I went a few minutes without thinking about him. This would inevitably lead me to start thinking about him again. A vicious cycle that got easier and easier as the days passed.

In time, my thoughts of him decreased from every day to every few days. I got easier the less contact I had from him.

After he realized how serious I was that it was over, he stopped calling. No warning. Just stopped. Can't say I blame him, but it still hurt.

He surprised me by calling out of the blue three days ago. I almost didn't recognize his voice.

"You letting your hair grow back?"

A deep voice startled me. I turned around and my heart skipped a beat. It was Cameron. He was coming out of a black Navigator, two vehicles from my car. This was his new vehicle, I assumed. The one he always told me he was going to get.

I wondered how long he had been watching me. How did I look to him, nervously scanning the area?

He looked the same. Except his eyes. They looked a little older. Sadder. Or maybe just tired. It was wishful thinking to believe he's spent countless sleepless nights since I left.

I finger-combed my shag hoping I looked better than he remembered. Secretly, I wanted him to miss me now as much as I used to miss him.

"Yeah. It was time for a change. The evolution of a new Nia." I touched my hair again. "It's growing back quicker than I expected, though. Can barely keep up the style."

"It looks good on you. You look good." He looked me up and down pausing at my breasts and hips. I was suddenly very conscious of the five pounds I had put on since the summer. I grabbed the sides of my blazer and pulled them closer to cover some of the extra weight.

"Actually, you look beautiful. More beautiful than the last time I saw you. Can I still get a hug?"

I reached on my tippy-toes and put my arms around his neck. He slipped his around my waist and pulled me close. His hug was firm but gentle – the heat from his body adding to the heat from this unusually warm winter day. I could feel perspiration break out across the bridge of my nose. It was December, but almost 80 degrees.

"Indian summer," my Gramma used to call this. Pneumonia weather.

"I don't care how warm it is, you make sure dat gurl wears her undershirt and her coat outside. This is pneumonia weather."

Hearing her voice in my memories calmed my spirit. *"Peace, be still,"* she would say. The butterflies in my stomach settled.

We let go of the hug and stared for a moment. He was in a plain white tee, jacket, and jeans. His chocolate complexion reflecting bronze highlights in the evening sun. His eyes carrying pain from recent loss. Even somber, he was still so handsome.

My heart started to race again. Feelings I thought I left behind this past summer, resurfaced. I had to resist the urge to hug him again. Kiss his full lips. Siphon some of his pain and make it mine.

I had to fight the urge to cry.

I looked away into the direction of the setting sun. The horizon was painted in beautiful reds, oranges, and purples. Planes took off across the sky every few minutes – one after the other. I wished that I were on one of them.

I imagined heading some place tropical and escaping Old Man Winter. The thought of the cold inevitably settling back in its rightful place of December made me sad.

At his request, I agreed to meet him at the BWI airport observation area. I figured families would be taking advantage of this gift from Mother Nature. Plenty of kids and plenty of open space. I didn't trust myself to meet him in a secluded place.

Children laughed and played on the small playground nearby trying to squeeze as much fun as they could out of what little daylight they had left. A little boy, about one year old, looked to the sky. He pointed and yelled excitedly at every passing plane. His parents watched nearby, tickled that he found so much joy in something so simple. Another child, running from her mother, fell on the concrete. Her wails causing heads to turn in unison as the mother rushed to console her.

My heart ached.

"So how have you been?" I tried to soften my tone a little.

He looked at me for a second and opened his mouth to say something. Then, probably thinking better of it, closed his mouth and glanced in the direction of the now quietly sobbing little girl. He looked at me and his game face was back on.

"Been good. Just working, eating, and trying to sleep."

"How's work?"

"Different. Not the same." He cleared his throat. "My new partner's cool. Funny. Dependable. Laid back. She goes harder than some of the dudes I know back home."

"*She?*" I thought. The green eyed-monster started to stir.

"She probably gets more pussy than they do, too." Unaware to my jealousy, he laughed. It felt good to hear him laugh.

I laughed, too, at my own stupid emotions.

His smile was beautiful.

"Damn, I miss Kevin."

He said this softly, and then looked into the sunset. The reflection illuminating the brown in his slanted eyes.

Eyes so small, they looked black.

"I know."

I looked in the same direction, allowing him a few seconds to reflect silently. His thoughts weren't with me. I had no place to interrupt them.

"So, what about you? You look good. Clothes. Hair. Body."

He looked me up and down again. His eyes expressed his approval of the new, fuller me.

Two of those extra pounds felt like they were in my breasts. My shirt felt uncomfortably tight.

"How are things in your world?"

"Things are going good. I started my own event planning business. It's called New Beginnings."

"Wow! So you finally decided to do it. I know your business is going to take off. It's definitely your niche."

"I hope so. I was scared, but I had to do it. It was now or never. I picked a career path to please my parents, but it wasn't for me. I still help Taz out with some things at work, since she hasn't found another office manager." I didn't mention all that had happened with Taz in the past few months. It wasn't his place to know.

"Oh, and I bought a townhouse in Columbia."

"So you and James got a place together,

huh? Guess you're definitely going to go through with getting mar-."

"We're not getting married." I cut him off before he could finish. "I called it off."

"Serious? Why?"

"Guess I wasn't ready." I didn't offer any more information.

He tried to maintain a neutral attitude, but his eyes betrayed him.

"Maybe he wasn't the one you were ready for."

He was right in that statement, but not in the implication. He seemed too happy at that moment, so I figured it was a chance to reopen old wounds.

"So how *is* Alicia?" Just mentioning her name made my insides wretch. Struggling to ignore the wave of nausea, I took a deep breath. But my eyes never left his. I didn't want him to think that I was still affected by anything he had done to me.

For the second time since we met, he looked uncomfortable. Awkwardly he answered.

"Well, um, she's...she's cool. I mean, she's doing okay. She's...it's, I mean the baby is due next month, on the 24th. They think maybe it's a girl. So..." He trailed off like he wasn't sure how much info to divulge.

"A girl?"

As much as I felt I had gotten over the whole situation, I obviously hadn't. His words dug up the hurt buried deep inside. A pain shot through my heart. My sinuses started to burn from the tears that threatening to come. Not wanting him to see my true feelings, I masked them with a fake smile.

"A girl? That's sweet." I tried not to sound

bitter, but it wasn't working. "I'm sure you two are very happy. Guess it was meant for you two to stay together, huh?"

"What?" He looked at me, confused.

"We're not together. I already told you, Nia, we weren't together when she got pregnant. It was over way before that. It's just that... she was always available whenever I called, no matter what time. I was too stupid and selfish to stop the physical part." He sighed with frustration. "We're not getting back together, and already, she's making me pay for it. One minute she's happy and talking to me about naming the baby after my mom and giving her my last name. The next, she's threatening never to let me even see my own child. Just this morning she said she won't let me be at the delivery. It's fucked up because I want to be a good father to my daughter, even though I'm not with her; but she won't see that. She just sees that I'm not with her." He gave a soft, humorless chuckle. "It's funny, but I never saw this side of her."

"You all never do."

Even though it still hurt to hear him talk about another woman having his baby, I still felt bad for him.

"I made a mistake by not being careful, but I'll never regret my child. I'll never be with Alicia, either. I knew I didn't want to be with her a long time ago. Hmmph, the way she's acting only confirms it."

He was emphasizing the whole we're-not-together-we'll-never-be-together thing too much for my benefit. Something in my expression must have told him that I didn't believe him because he sighed again, shook his head, and changed the subject.

"You know that kid who shot Kevin? He was convicted as a minor. Sentenced to six months in juvie and then home monitoring."

"I don't know, Cameron. It was an accident. Honestly, I don't think he should have gotten anything. I know Kevin was your friend and a cop, but that boy never meant to hurt anyone. He was just scared and trying to protect his mother."

He rubbed a hand over his face.

"I agree with you. He's already suffered more than he should have. But I'm just part of the system. I don't control it. The worst part is after all that, his mom never came out of that coma. She ended up dying in the hospital."

"Oh my God! Cameron that's awful!"

The thought of him losing his mother after everything he's been through was too much. The tears ran down without any resistance. Instinctively, he wrapped his strong arms around me and pulled me close to his chest - like he used to do. Rubbed my head in comfort.

"His uncle OD'd about 2 months ago. No other family member has come to claim him, so he's a ward of the state."

"Jesus! That poor boy! Oh Cameron, what's going to happen to him?"

"I petitioned the court to become his guardian."

I pulled away and looked up at him. "You did what?"

"I want to take him in as a foster child. Nia, this boy has so much potential, and I don't want him to get fucked up in the system. Me and so many of my friends never had our fathers around to raise us. Some of my friends are still messed up because of it. At least I had my mom to raise me the best she could to be a man. This kid has no one. No one, baby. I'm not letting him become another statistic. Some good is going to come out of this. If I can give this boy the love, security, and guidance he needs to become a productive young man, not some degenerate like the losers I see every day, then maybe...maybe Kevin's death won't be in vain."

Voice choking with his last sentence, he looked away.

I found a new level of respect for this man I loved.

I still love him.

I gently touched his chest to catch his attention. "Are you sure about this?" I asked softly.

"Never been more sure about anything else in my life...except you."

It didn't sound like a line. His feelings seemed genuine. I could see that in the way his eyes pleaded with mine for forgiveness.

I really wanted to hug him again and tell him everything that's been on my heart, but my stubbornness prevailed.

Getting no response, he sighed again and let that statement float away in the warm winter breeze.

"Sometimes, it doesn't seem real that he's gone. Once in awhile, I'll have a dream about him. We're laughing and joking like when we were kids. I can feel myself smiling in my sleep. Then, I wake up and reality settles; so does that feeling in the pit of my stomach."

I didn't really know what to say to him at that moment to ease his pain, so I didn't try.

"You know, as much as it hurt when Kevin died. I felt the same pain when you walked out of my life, Nia. When I lost you, I lost a piece of myself."

I understood that kind of loss.

I don't know why I felt more for him after a one-year affair, than I did for James after a seven-year relationship. If ever there were such a thing as soul mates, we were probably it.

But I didn't believe in such things.

"I lost something, too."

I took the fingers of my right hand and touched the area over my heart to send a message. If I said too much right now, I'd start crying; so I didn't. If I could say something, it would be how much I wanted him to hold me again; but I couldn't.

As if reading my mind, he grabbed me. Held me so tight, it startled me. Then, I relaxed and let him hold me. I let him rock me in a slight side-to-side motion.

"I'll never forgive myself for fucking up with you."

So much hurt.

My heart, heavy.

My tears, heavy.

I let them fall.

"I still love you."

Those four words, whispered in my ear, pulled at my heart so forcefully, I had to fight every fiber within to keep from breaking down.

"I know."

I wanted to tell him that I still loved him, too, but the hurt from his betrayal was too fresh.

I couldn't let it go. I let the truth in that statement remain one-sided.

He released me after a few more minutes, and I pulled myself together.

"I have to go, Sweetheart, before I pick you

up and take you with me."

Hands as big as my face, caressed my cheek. Sending tingles where he touched.

"I don't want to go, but I have to."

"I understand."

He waited for a few seconds to see if I had anything else to offer him.

I didn't.

"Bye, babygirl. I know what you told me, but if you ever need anything...if you change your mind, you know my number."

"I know."

"At least call every so often. Let me know how you're doing."

"Maybe."

But I didn't think I would.

Steel walls encased my heart once more.

I went back to being cordial.

He acknowledged defeat and walked to his truck. Using that confident stroll that I loved so much. As soon as he got in, the butterflies started again.

I wanted to call out his name, but couldn't.

"Please don't go." I pleaded with him in my mind. *"Hold me. Tell me you're sorry over and over again. Beg me to give you another chance. Prove to me I can trust you. Should trust you."*

As if he heard my mental anguish, he looked at me; but, the only thing he did was kiss his two fingers, and then use them to touch the window.

I did the same to the air

My mouth wouldn't open. Pride and pain kept it sealed. Even if I could, the words were already caught in the oversized lump in my throat. I swallowed hard trying not to choke on them.

As he drove off, I followed his truck with

my eyes until he cruised out of my visual field.

The butterflies danced in a frenzy until I thought I would faint.

I put my hand on my stomach and spoke quietly.

"Shhh. I know, but I need to be by myself for right now. You'll be okay with me."

I sighed and a heavy tear rolled down my cheek.

"We'll be okay with each other."

The flutter in my womb seemed to think otherwise because it continued to move as if in protest.

Questioning for the first time my decision to keep Cameron out of my life, I rubbed my stomach some more and said, "I know. I'm sorry."

The flutter settled down at my admission – content to have this small victory. I looked at the kids on the playground then, looked back in the direction that Cameron went. I stared at the empty horizon.

Who knows? Maybe it'll all be too much. Maybe going to the doctor by myself will get to be too lonely.

Maybe feeling a twinge and seeing a foot press out of my swollen abdomen will make me wish for the strong hand of its father.

To share the experience.

To accompany me in a miracle.

Maybe if I gain a little nerve and lose a lot of pride, I'll call him.

For now though, it's just me and my growing belly. I have a new life to think about.

A new beginning.

But in time...

"Just maybe..."

I stared down at the sleeping figure in my arms. Soft black curls. Downy, tan skin. Dimples. Unbelievably long eyelashes.

I inhaled the sweet air escaping from his open mouth. His breathing was even. Rhythmic.

Unable to resist, I kissed the very tip of his nose.

He stirred in my arms, but didn't wake.

My heart swelled from the fierce love it contained. Love for this tiny, helpless life. I never thought I could feel so much joy for something so small.

"All right, give him up. It's my turn to hold him."

Before I could respond, she reached down and pried him from my arms.

"Look at grandma's baby! So pretty!"

"Mom, he's a boy. He's not pretty; he's handsome."

"Oh, whatever! He's gorgeous!"

She transformed, as she always did, when she held him. The tough, no-nonsense woman that I had known all my life turned into a big softy when she held her only grandson.

"Ohhhhh, Grandmommy missed her baby boy!"

She put her face into his chubby neck and sniffed loudly.

"Mmmmm. Smells so good."

"Come on, Ma! Auntie wants to hold her little man, too."

Standing in her black stretch pants, minidress, and stiletto boots, my baby sister didn't look as if she was dressed to play with babies.

She grew impatient and tried to quickly scoop my son from his grandmother's arms.

She was unsuccessful.

Nikia usually came along with my mother to visit. Sometimes, they would stay for an hour. Sometimes, they wouldn't leave until the next day.

This was becoming a weekly routine.

Having to settle with only being able to touch her nephew, she gently grabbed a chubby fist and stroked the skin of his arm with her thumb.

"Why is he still so light, Nee-Nee? You sure this is Cameron's baby?"

My mom shot Nikia a nasty look and went back to rocking her grandchild.

I glared at her. My expression let her know that I didn't want to hear anymore.

Unfazed by us both, she kept going.

"What? I'm just saying. Cameron is dark-skinned. He should have gotten some more color by now."

Like my mother, Nikia was never one to hold her tongue. Unfortunately, for those around her, she lacked any of our mother's tact or timing.

"Daddy was dark-skinned, and look at us."

"Daddy was brown-skinned. Cameron is damn near black. But CJ is lighter than me," She glanced at our mom for some sign of support before she continued. Mommy kept her eyes to her grandchild as Nikia pressed on. "He's the same complexion as James. And he has dimples, Nee, just like James. You don't have dimples. Cameron doesn't have dimples..."

"But you do and so does Mommy. We're not going back and forth about this again. I told you already. I know who my son's father is."

But did I really?

Before talking to Taz, I was certain I had my period between the last time I had sex with James and the last time I slept with Cameron.

"Are you sure it was a regular period?" she had asked me. Then, I remembered it was two days shorter than normal. I had messed up on my pills so bad, that I had to start over. Except, stress and mild depression had made me forget to do just that. And I had slept with two lovers, without protection, within the same month.

The fact that Cameron II was born two weeks before his due date, weighing 8 lbs and 6 oz, only added to my nagging doubt.

Despite all of the circumstances surrounding his conception, I know in my heart he's Cameron's. I knew the moment I realized I was pregnant.

I don't care what anyone thinks.

Seeing this as a good time to break the news to me, my mom interrupted.

"You know, James came by the house last Tuesday."

My mom watches CJ for me while I work.

"What? Why didn't you tell me? You didn't let him see Cameron, did you?"

I hadn't seen James since last fall.

I told him that I was pregnant and that it wasn't his. He didn't believe me. Said I was doing this just to get him back for hurting me. I thought that statement alone would make him go away.

It didn't.

After repeated calls, begging me for another chance, I changed my number.

After numerous unannounced visits to my apartment, bearing gifts and tears, I moved without letting him know where.

I forbade my family and friends from giving him any of my information under penalty of disownment.

"Niani, he truly believes he's Cameron's father."

"Did you let him see Cameron?" There was tension in my voice. A tight feeling began forming at my temples. I was starting to get a headache.

"I did. You won't talk to him. You've forbidden any of us to give him your new address or phone number."

I was so irritated, that I couldn't look in her direction.

"Don't be mad, Nia, but he wanted to hold him."

I glared at her – shooting anger, sharp as daggers, from my eyes.

She didn't flinch.

"You didn't let him—?"

"I couldn't say no to him. Baby, he looked so sad. If you saw the way he was looking at CJ, you couldn't have denied him, either. You should have seen him holding CJ."

I couldn't believe what I was hearing. My face got hot. I was so mad, tears threatened to form. My vision turned misty red.

"He wants to you to get a DNA test to prove to you that he's the father."

I would never disrespect my mother, but I so badly wanted to snatch my son back and kick both of her and my sister out of my house. I grit my teeth, trying to contain my emotions.

Then, she said something that set me off.

"He does resemble James a little..."

That was the last straw. I couldn't take it. I exploded in fury.

"Stop saying that! Yes, they have similar complexions and dimples, and they both have a penis, but the similarities end there! He's got Cameron's eyes! His nose! Even his hairline! Almost the same exact face, save for his mouth, which is mine!"

Nikia's eyes widened with surprise. She stepped to side, as if moving out of the way of a potential blow – from either side.

My mother's expression never changed.

"I know who CJ's father is!"

But did I really?

My mother looked at her oldest daughter and frowned. Her expression was still serious, but now merged with sadness.

It caught me off guard.

She looked down at her grandchild who had awakened and was staring quietly. Tenderly, she rubbed his head—careful to avoid the soft spot—and looked back at me.

She sighed.

"Then, take the test."